Victoria And Vancouver Island Travel Guide

2024-2025

Explore The Sophisticated Capital Of British Columbia And Rain City With Maps And Photos

Glynn S. Thompson

Copyright

Table of Contents

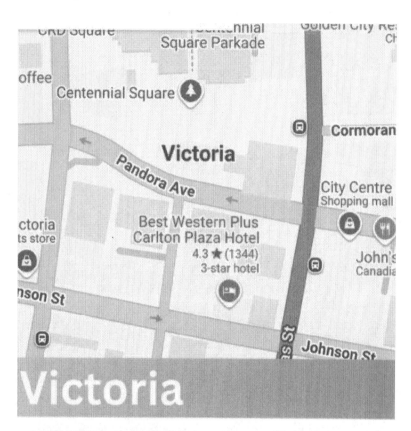

Scan the QR code

1. Open Camera: Launch your smartphone's camera app.

2. Position QR Code: Place the QR code within the camera's viewfinder.

3. Hold Steady: Keep the device steady for the camera to focus.

4. Wait for Scan: Wait for the code to be recognized.

5. Tap Notification: Follow the prompt to access the content.

6

SECTION I: VICTORIA

Chapter 1. Introduction

Welcome to Vancouver Island and Victoria

Greetings from Vancouver Island and Victoria's magical world! A symphony of the beauty of nature and a vibrant tapestry of culture and history greet me as soon as I set foot on this lovely land.

Victoria, the sophisticated capital of British Columbia, enthrals with its vibrant Inner Harbor, rich gardens, and charming architecture. I strolled around the old streets, taking in the vibrant homes and the famous Parliament Buildings. The Butchart Gardens, where a kaleidoscope of flowers flowered in spectacular grandeur, was a dream come true.

From First Nations artefacts to displays of marine life, the Royal BC Museum provided an enthralling look into the rich history of the area.

I set out on an adventure around the delights of Vancouver Island after leaving Victoria. With its immaculate beaches, tall rainforests, and a wealth of species, the Pacific Rim National Park Reserve was a sanctuary for those who loved the outdoors. I hiked into Cathedral Grove's old groves, where I was astounded by the tall Douglas firs, and I explored Tofino's rocky beach, where surfers rode the strong waves.

Everywhere on the island, one could see the diversity of cultures. I enjoyed local craft beer at a busy brewery, ate delicious seafood at a small seaside restaurant, and saw the lively First Nations culture at a totem pole park.

I am incredibly thankful for the life-changing experiences I had while travelling through Victoria and Vancouver Island. This charming place has made a lasting impression on me, from the tranquil beauty of the surroundings to the friendly greetings of the locals.

Glynn S. Thompson.

Chapter 2. Points of Interest

Butchart Gardens

A must-see location in Victoria, British Columbia, is the Butchart Gardens, a masterwork of horticultural craftsmanship. A kaleidoscope of hues and fragrances will greet you as soon as you enter this colourful haven.

Things to Investigate:

- **The Garden in the Sunken**: Once a limestone quarry, this gorgeous garden is no longer a magnificent exhibition of blooming splendour. Discover colourful flower beds, calm ponds, and meandering walkways.
- **The Rose Garden**: Thousands of roses in bloom create a beautiful scene in this fragrant retreat.
- **The Japanese Garden**: A peaceful haven with peaceful ponds, bridges, and well-kept gardens that provide an insight into Japanese culture.
- **The Italian Garden**: This garden, which was influenced by the Renaissance, has statues, fountains, and formal geometric forms.
- **TMediterranean landscape**: Succulents, cacti, and drought-tolerant plants in a sun-drenched landscape.

Cost: The cost of tickets varies according to the season. The official Butchart Gardens website allows you to view the most recent costs.

Scan the QR code

1. Open Camera: Launch your smartphone's camera app.
2. Position QR Code: Place the QR code within the camera's viewfinder.
3. Hold Steady: Keep the device steady for the camera to focus.
4. Wait for Scan: Wait for the code to be recognized.
5. Tap Notification: Follow the prompt to access the content.

How to Get There:

- **By Car**: Driving to the Butchart Gardens is simple. It takes about twenty minutes to go to Victoria's downtown.
- **By Bus**: A number of bus operators provide Butchart Gardens trips. For precise information and schedules, you can inquire with nearby tour providers.

The Royal BC Museum

A fascinating exploration of the rich history and varied cultures of British Columbia may be found in the Royal BC Museum.

Things to Investigate:

- Explore relics, stories, and artwork in the First Peoples Gallery to get a deeper understanding of the rich cultures of First Nations peoples.
- Explore the wonders of nature, from marine life to ancient species, at the Natural History Gallery.
- **Historic Villages**: Recreated streets and buildings allow visitors to travel back in time and experience life in British Columbia in the 19th century.
- **Special Exhibitions**: Take in a range of transient displays that highlight science, art, and history from throughout the globe.

Price:

Seasons and special exhibitions have an impact on ticket costs. The Royal BC Museum's website allows you to view the most recent prices.

How to Get There:

- In the heart of Victoria, British Columbia stands the Royal BC Museum. You can get there by car, bus, or foot with ease. To get to the museum, you can also enjoy a beautiful stroll along the shoreline.

Craigdarroch Castle

A stunning home from the Victorian era, Craigdarroch Castle provides a window into the lavish way of life of the 19th century.

Things to Investigate:

Explore the castle's vast rooms, which include the magnificent library, the sumptuous dining room, and the exquisite drawing room.

- **Architectural Details**: Take in the castle's interior decorations, which include elaborate woodwork, stained glass windows, and elaborate fireplaces.
- **Tower**: For sweeping views of Victoria and the **surroundings**, ascend the castle's tower.

Cost: The cost of tickets varies according to the season. The Craigdarroch Castle website allows you to view the most recent prices.

How to Get There:

- British Columbia's Victoria is home to Craigdarroch Castle. You may get there by bus or automobile with ease. The castle is also accessible by foot from Victoria's downtown.

Parliament Buildings in British Columbia

An iconic representation of British Columbia's past, the Parliament Buildings are a magnificent example of Victorian architecture.

Things to Investigate:

- **Grand Architecture**: Take in the striking exterior, elaborate accents, and the imposing central dome.
- **Free Guided Tours**: Learn about the legislative process and the building's history by taking a free guided tour.
- **Legislative Assembly**: Attend sessions of the legislature from the public gallery (time permitting).
- Enjoy a dinner in the Parliamentary Dining Room, a historic space with breathtaking views of the Inner Harbor.

Cost: There is no charge to enter the Parliament Buildings. On the other hand, exceptional events and dining experiences could incur fees.

How to Get There:

- Victoria, British Columbia's downtown is home to the Parliament Buildings. By car, bus, or foot, they are easily accessible. To get to the buildings, you can also take a beautiful stroll along the waterfront.

Beacon Hill Park

In the centre of Victoria sits Beacon Hill Park, a vast natural beauty haven.

Things to Investigate:

- Explore the park's well-kept gardens, verdant meadows, and meandering paths.
- **Encounters with Wildlife**: Look for the park's resident ducks, peacocks, and other animals.
- **Playgrounds and Picnic Areas**: Take advantage of family-friendly attractions including a petting zoo, picnic areas, and playgrounds.
- **Shoreline**: Unwind by the shoreline while admiring breathtaking views of the Juan de Fuca Strait.

Cost: There is no charge to enter Beacon Hill Park.

Scan the QR code

1. Open Camera: Launch your smartphone's camera app.

2. Position QR Code: Place the QR code within the camera's viewfinder.

3. Hold Steady: Keep the device steady for the camera to focus.

4. Wait for Scan: Wait for the code to be recognized.

5. Tap Notification: Follow the prompt to access the content.

How to Get There:

- Beacon Hill Park is ideally situated in Victoria's downtown. You can easily get there by foot, by bicycle, or by public transit.

The Fisherman's Wharf

Victoria's Fisherman's Wharf is a bustling waterfront destination that offers a distinctive fusion of local shops, mouthwatering cuisine, and marine life.

Things to Investigate:

Admire the vibrant and eccentric float houses that line the shoreline.

- **Wildlife Observation**: Look for amusing seals, sea otters, and other aquatic animals.
- **Local Stores**: Look through distinctive stores that offer artwork, souvenirs, and regional goods.
- **Fresh Seafood**: Savour mouthwatering seafood meals at one of the many eateries along the shore.

Cost: There is no charge to enter Fisherman's Wharf. However, you might have to pay for things like whale-watching tours, eating, and shopping.

How to Get There:

- Victoria's Inner Harbour is only a short stroll from Fisherman's Wharf. It's easily accessible by foot or a quick bus journey.

Chinatown

Chinatown in Victoria is a fascinating historical neighbourhood that offers a wealth of distinctive experiences and cultural charm.

Things to Investigate:

Enter Fan Tan Alley, Canada's tiniest street, which is lined with vibrant stores and restaurants.

- **Chinese Gate**: Take in this famous entryway to Chinatown's elaborate sculptures and vivid hues.
- Explore the beautifully conserved old structures, such as the Chinese Freemasons Hall and the Chinese Public School.
- **Local Stores**: Visit the local stores to find fresh produce, traditional Chinese products, and unusual gifts.
- **Real Food**: Savour delectable Chinese dishes, such as dim sum, noodles, and barbecue.

Cost: There is no charge to enter Chinatown. However, you might have to pay for guided excursions, lunch, and shopping.

How to Get There:

- Chinatown is situated in the centre of Victoria's downtown. It's simple to get to by vehicle, foot, or public transit.

The Inner Harbor

With its breathtaking waterfront vistas, historic sites, and lively ambiance, Victoria's Inner Harbour is the city's pulsating centre.

Things to Investigate:

- **Parliament Buildings**: Enjoy a complimentary guided tour and marvel at the striking architecture of these famous structures.

- Admire the magnificence of the Empress Hotel, a historic establishment renowned for its sophisticated atmosphere and afternoon tea.
- **Royal BC Museum**: Explore British Columbia's natural beauty and rich history at this top-notch museum.
- **Waterfront**: Take in the vibrant ambiance while strolling around the waterfront and seeing the boats and seaplanes.
- **Shopping & Dining**: Take advantage of the many souvenirs and delectable food available at the stores and eateries that line the Inner Harbor.

Cost: There is no charge to enter the Inner Harbor. However, admission to the museum, dining, and shopping may incur expenses.

How to Get There:

- Easily reachable by foot, vehicle, or public transportation, the Inner Harbour is situated in Victoria's downtown. A lot of the sights may be reached by foot from one another.

Chapter 3. Activities

Whale Watching

The following are some well-known whale-watching trip companies in Vancouver Island, British Columbia:

Tours on Eagle Wings

Where: Leaves from Victoria's Inner Harbor

- To make a reservation, visit https://www.eaglewingtours.com/
- The price varies based on the tour. For the most recent prices, see their website.
- **How to Get There**: It is simple to get to the departure location by vehicle, foot, or public transit.

Whale Watch on Vancouver Island

Location: Leaves Nanaimo Harbor

- http://www.vancouverislandwhalewatch.com/ How to Make a Reservation

- The price varies based on the tour. For the most recent prices, see their website.
- **How to Get There**: Driving or taking public transit to the departure place is simple.

Adventures with Marine Wildlife and Whales at Prince of Whales

Where: Leaves from Victoria's Inner Harbor

- https://princeofwhales.com/vancouver-whale-watching/ is the booking link.

- The price varies based on the tour. For the most recent prices, see their website.
- **How to Get There**: You can easily get to the departure point by vehicle, foot, or public transportation.

Ocean EcoVentures

Where: Leaves Parksville or Cowichan Bay

- Visit https://oceanecoventures.com/ to make a reservation.

- The price varies based on the tour. For the most recent prices, see their website.
- **How to Get There**: You can take public transit or drive to the departure locations.

Spirit Adventures with Orcas

Location: Leaves Nanaimo Harbor

- The booking link is https://orcaspirit.com/.

- The price varies based on the tour. For the most recent prices, see their website.
- **How to Get There**: Driving or taking public transit to the departure place is simple.

Aircraft Excursions

A few well-known seaplane tour companies in Victoria, British Columbia, are as follows:

Seaplanes operated by Harbour Air

To make a reservation, visit

- https://www.harbourair.com/

- The price varies based on the tour. For the most recent prices, see their website.

Spirit Adventures with Orcas

- The booking link is https://orcaspirit.com/.

- The price varies based on the tour. For the most recent prices, see their website.

Whale Watching in the Spring

- The price varies based on the tour. For the most recent prices, see their website.

Shopping in Victoria is varied and includes everything from high-end malls to local markets and small stores. Here are a few well-liked locations for shopping:

Victoria's Downtown:

- **Government Boulevard**: There are stores, boutiques, and art galleries lining this famous boulevard.
- **Market plaza**: A quaint old plaza with distinctive stores, cafes, and eateries.
- Explore the waterfront stores in the inner harbour, which provide seafood, handicrafts, and souvenirs.
- **Malls**: Mayfair Shopping Centre: A sizable shopping centre including a range of shops, including both local boutiques and well-known brands.
- A mix of department stores and niche shops can be found at The Bay Centre, a downtown retail centre.

Local Markets:

- **Esquimalt Farmers' Market:** A bustling marketplace including regional food sellers, handmade goods, and fresh produce.
- Smaller markets that sell regional food, handicrafts, and baked goods are Breakwater Market and James Bay Community Market.

Other Retail Areas:

- Cadboro Bay Village is a charming retail area with distinctive cafes and boutiques.

- **Oak Bay Village**: A quaint community with high-end stores and eateries.

How to Get There: In Victoria's downtown, the majority of these shopping destinations are accessible by foot. You may easily travel by vehicle, taxi, or public transportation to the main malls or marketplaces located outside of downtown.

Museums And Art Galleries

Greater Victoria Art Gallery

Located in the centre of Victoria, British Columbia, the Art Gallery of Greater Victoria (AGGV) is a cultural treasure.

Things to Investigate:

- **Diverse Collection of Art:** Discover a variety of art forms, such as paintings, sculptures, and photographs, ranging from historical to modern.
- **Special Exhibitions**: Take in the temporary displays of regional, national, and worldwide artists.
- **Spencer Mansion**: Travel back in time and take in this historic mansion's stunning Victorian architecture.
- **Educational Programs**: Take part in family-friendly events, seminars, and lectures.

Cost: Depending on the exhibitions and activities, different admission costs apply. For the most recent pricing details, see the AGGV website.

How to Get There:

- The AGGV is situated in Victoria's Rockland neighbourhood. Getting there by vehicle or public transit is simple. To get to the gallery, you can also go for a beautiful bike ride or stroll.

British Columbia's Maritime Museum

Offering a fascinating look into the rich nautical history of the Pacific Northwest, the nautical Museum of British Columbia is a veritable gold mine for those who enjoy the sea.

Things to Investigate:

- **Interesting Exhibits:** Explore interactive displays that highlight the history of seafaring, shipbuilding, and exploration.
- **Historic items**: Examine a variety of maritime items, such as ship models, navigational aids, and the personal effects of well-known adventurers.
- **First Nations Maritime Culture**: Through displays on traditional canoes, fishing methods, and cultural customs, discover the close ties that First Nations peoples have to the ocean.
- **Special Exhibitions**: Take in short-term displays that focus on particular subjects, such as shipwrecks, underwater archaeology, or marine art.

Cost: Depending on the exhibitions and activities, different admission costs apply. For the most recent information on prices, see the Maritime Museum of British Columbia website.

How to Get There:

- Downtown Victoria, British Columbia, is home to the Maritime Museum of British Columbia. Getting there via vehicle, public transit, or foot is simple. To get to the museum, you can also enjoy a beautiful stroll along the shoreline.

Biking and Hiking

From modest walks to strenuous mountain bike courses, Victoria has a wide range of hiking and riding paths. Here are a few well-liked choices:

Hiking Beacon Hill Park:

- **How to Get There:** This park is conveniently located in Victoria's downtown and is reachable by bicycle or foot.

Galloping Goose Trail:

- **How to Get There:** It begins close to Victoria's Inner Harbor and is free. Accessible via public transportation, bicycle, or automobile.
- Mount Douglas Park is **free** to enter. It is situated in Saanich, just a short drive from Victoria. Accessible by bus or automobile.
- Biking is free.
- The Galloping Goose Trail begins close to Victoria's Inner Harbour. Accessible via public transportation, bicycle, or automobile.

The Lochside Trail is free to use.

Directions: It begins close to Victoria's Inner Harbour. Accessible via public transportation, bicycle, or automobile.

- The Hartford Mountain Bike Park is free to enter.
- Directions: It's close to Saanich. Car-accessible.
- Topaz Park is free.
- **Directions**: It's in Victoria. Accessible via public transportation, bicycle, or automobile.

Cost: Free Bike Rentals: There are several bike stores in Victoria where you can hire bikes, including:

The Bicycle Store

Cycle Solutions Spokes Bicycle Shop

Chapter 4. Travel Itinerary

A Week-long Journey

Day 1: Arrival and Exploration of the Inner Harbor

- **Morning**: Check into your hotel after landing at Victoria International Airport.

- **Afternoon**: stroll around the magnificent Inner Harbor, admiring the imposing Empress Hotel and the famous Parliament Buildings.

- **Evening**: Take a walk around the waterfront after a leisurely meal at a restaurant near the water.

Day 2: Royal BC Museum and Butchart Gardens

- **Morning**: Take in the magnificent display of flowers at the world-famous Butchart Gardens.

- **Afternoon**: Visit the Royal BC Museum to learn about British Columbia's history and culture.

- **Evening**: Have a laid-back meal at a brewery or bar in the area.

Day 3: Adventure with Whale Watching

- **Morning**: From the Inner Harbor, set out on a whale-watching excursion.

- **Afternoon**: Take in the vibrant float houses and stroll around the quaint Fisherman's Wharf.

- **Evening**: Savour the lively nightlife while dining at a restaurant on the water.

Day 4: Exploration Outside

- **Morning**: Take a hike along one of Mount Douglas Park or Beacon Hill Park's picturesque trails.

- **Afternoon**: take a bike ride on the well-travelled Galloping Goose Trail.

- **Evening**: Unwind at a nearby spa or savour a home-cooked meal at a farm-to-table eatery.

Day 5: Day Trip to an Island

- **Morning**: Visit the quaint town of Victoria after taking a ferry to Vancouver Island.

- **Afternoon**: take in the breathtaking Butchart Gardens or the old Craigdarroch Castle.

- **Evening**: Head back to Victoria and savour a delectable meal at a neighbourhood eatery.

Day 6: Immersion in Culture

- **Morning**: Take in the varied collection of artwork at the Art Gallery of Greater Victoria.

- **Afternoon**: Take a tour of Chinatown, a bustling area with distinctive stores and eateries.

- **Evening**: Take in a live music performance at a nearby location or see a show at the McPherson Playhouse.

Day 7: Leaving

- **Morning**: gather your belongings and depart from your lodging.

- **Afternoon**: have your last supper at a favourite restaurant or take one more look around the city.

- **Evening:** Depart from Victoria International Airport in the evening.

Advice for Your Journey:

- **Best Time to Go**: The weather is nice for outdoor activities throughout the spring and summer.
- **Accommodations**: Take into account booking a room in a contemporary hotel, a boutique inn, or a historic hotel.
- **Transportation**: To get to the island, rent a car or take public transit.
- **Packing**: Bring sunscreen, rain gear, and comfy clothes.
- **Budget**: Make a budget that accounts for lodging, meals, travel, and entertainment.

Chapter 5. Accommodations

The Fairmont Empress Hotel

A historic landmark in Victoria, the Fairmont Empress Hotel is renowned for its exquisite architecture and opulent lodgings. It is a well-liked tourist attraction in Victoria and provides breathtaking views of the Inner Harbor.

Cost: The type of accommodation, time of year, and availability all affect how much a stay at the Fairmont Empress costs. For up-to-date pricing and reservation details, it is advised to visit their website.

How to Get There:

Victoria, British Columbia's downtown is home to the Fairmont Empress Hotel. Getting there by vehicle, taxi, or public transit is simple.

Victoria Regent Hotel

In the centre of Victoria's city stands the opulent waterfront Victoria Regent Hotel. It is renowned for its cosy lodgings and handy location, and it provides breathtaking views of the Inner Harbor.

Cost: The type of accommodation, time of year, and availability all affect how much a stay at the Victoria Regent Hotel costs. For up-to-date pricing and reservation details, it is advised to visit their website.

How to Get There:

In the heart of Victoria, British Columbia sits the Victoria Regent Hotel. Getting there by vehicle, taxi, or public transit is simple.

The Magnolia Spa & Hotel

In the centre of Victoria's city stands the opulent boutique hotel known as the Magnolia Hotel & Spa. It provides a comfortable and fashionable stay by combining contemporary conveniences with traditional elegance.

Cost: The type of room, time of year, and availability all affect how much a stay at the Magnolia Hotel & Spa costs. For up-to-date pricing and reservation details, it is advised to visit their website.

How to Get There:

Victoria, British Columbia's downtown is home to the Magnolia Hotel & Spa. It is conveniently reachable by vehicle, taxi, or public transit.

Chapter 6. Meals

Seafood

Victoria is known for having a wide variety of fresh seafood. There will likely be a range of meals made with regional seafood, including:

Salmon: Victoria offers a range of salmon meals, such as smoked salmon, grilled salmon, and salmon burgers, made from farmed Atlantic salmon as well as wild-caught sockeye.

A favourite option for fish and chips, grilled fish, and seafood chowder is halibut, a firm, white fish.

Crab: A specialty of the area, Dungeness crab is frequently served steamed or in crab cakes.

Fresh oysters, which may be eaten raw or cooked in a variety of ways, are a must-try in Victoria.

Clams and mussels are shellfish that are frequently used in steamed pots, pasta meals, and seafood chowders.

Depending on the restaurant, the dish, and the freshness of the materials, seafood dishes in Victoria can range greatly in price. On the other hand, fresh, locally-produced seafood is typically more expensive.

Cafés and Restaurants

Pizza Pagliacci's

A well-known institution in Victoria, Pagliacci's Pizza is renowned for its flavorful wood-fired pizzas, substantial pasta meals, and vibrant environment. Both locals and visitors find it to be a popular location.

How to Get There:

Pagliacci's is situated on Broad Street in the heart of Victoria. It's simple to get to by vehicle, foot, or public transit.

The Terrazzo

A well-known Italian eatery in Victoria, British Columbia, Il Terrazzo is praised for its genuine food, welcoming ambiance, and wide selection of wines. It is housed in a historic structure with a lovely courtyard.

How to Get There:

Il Terrazzo is situated just off Johnson Street on Waddington Alley in the heart of Victoria. It's simple to get to by vehicle or foot.

Finn's Cocktails, Seafood, and Chops

A well-liked waterfront eatery in Victoria, British Columbia, Finn's Seafood, Chops, and Cocktails is renowned for its prime steaks, fresh seafood, and traditional cocktails. It is located in a historic structure with breathtaking Inner Harbor views.

How to Get There:

Wharf Street in the heart of Victoria is home to Finn's Seafood, Chops, and Cocktails. It's simple to get to by vehicle, foot, or public transit.

Chapter 7. Historical and Cultural Context

The Provincial Museum of British Columbia

In the centre of Victoria, British Columbia sits the world-renowned Royal BC Museum. It contains an extensive collection of specimens, artefacts, and historical records that highlight the province's natural beauty and rich history.

Things to Investigate:

- Explore British Columbia's varied ecosystems from the coast to the mountains in the Natural History Gallery.
- Explore relics, stories, and artwork in the First Peoples Gallery to get a deeper understanding of the many cultures of First Nations peoples.
- **Historic Villages**: Recreated streets and buildings allow visitors to travel back in time and experience life in British Columbia in the 19th century.
- **Special Exhibitions**: Take in a range of transient displays that highlight science, art, and history from throughout the globe.

Price:

- The cost of admission varies according to the events and exhibitions. For the most recent information on prices, see the Royal BC Museum website.

How to Get There:

- Downtown Victoria's Belleville Street is home to the Royal BC Museum. It is easily accessible by car, bus, or on foot.

Fort Rodd Hill National Historic Site

Fort Rodd Hill National Historic Site is a 19th-century coastal artillery fort located on the Colwood side of Esquimalt Harbour, in Victoria. It offers tourists an insight into Canada's military history.

Things to Investigate:

- **19th-century Artillery Fort**: Explore the well-preserved fortifications, including gun batteries, underground storage, and command stations.
- **Lighthouse**: Visit the neighbouring Fisgard Lighthouse, the oldest lighthouse on Canada's West Coast.
- **Beautiful paths**: Hike along the park's beautiful paths, affording stunning views of the ocean and surrounding environment.
- **Picnic Areas**: Relax and have a picnic amidst the natural beauty of the park.

Price:

- Admission fees may apply. For the most recent pricing details, see the Parks Canada website.

How to Get There:

- About 20 minutes drive from Victoria's downtown lies Fort Rodd Hill, which is situated on the city's outskirts. By car, it's easily accessible. Public transit can also take you to the fort, albeit it might involve taking a bus and walking.

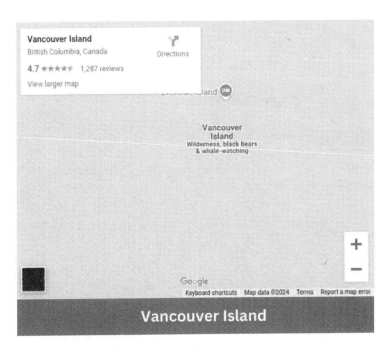

Vancouver Island
British Columbia, Canada

4.7 ★★★★½ 1,287 reviews

View larger map

Vancouver Island
Wilderness, black bears
& whale-watching

Vancouver Island

SCAN THE QR CODE

1. Open your device's camera app.
2. Point the camera at the QR code.
3. Hold steady and wait for recognition.
4. Review the displayed information.
5. Follow the prompt to access the content.

SECTION 2: VANCOUVER ISLAND

Chapter 1. Points of Interest

Pacific Rim National Park Reserve

The west coast of Vancouver Island, British Columbia, is home to the breathtaking Pacific Rim National Park Reserve. With a wide variety of activities and stunning landscapes, it's a paradise for outdoor lovers.

Things to Investigate:

- **Long Beach**: An exquisite section of sandy shoreline ideal for beachcombing, surfing, and tanning.
- With more than 100 islands, Broken Group Islands is a kayaker's paradise with chances to camp, see animals, and explore tide pools.
- The West Coast Trail is a strenuous multi-day hiking route renowned for its untamed landscape, breathtaking coastline vistas, and distinctive ecological characteristics.

Price:

- There is a cost to enter the park. For the most recent pricing details, see the Parks Canada website.

How to Get There:

- The west coast of Vancouver Island is home to Pacific Rim National Park Reserve. Tofino and Ucluelet are the nearest major towns and are accessible by ferry or automobile. You may drive, bike, or walk to various areas of the park if you're in Tofino or Ucluelet.

Cathedral Grove

Situated in MacMillan Provincial Park on Vancouver Island in British Columbia, Canada, Cathedral Grove is a mystical woodland. Ancient Douglas fir trees, some of which are more than 800 years old and more than 80 metres tall, are its most famous feature.

Things to Investigate:

- Explore a grove of massive Douglas fir trees, some of which are over 800 years old.

- **Scenic pathways**: Take a stroll along the old forest's network of pathways.
- **Possibilities for Photography**: Take breathtaking pictures of the huge trees and verdant woodland environs.

Price:

- Cathedral Grove is free to enter.

How to Get There:

- On Vancouver Island, Cathedral Grove is situated in MacMillan Provincial Park. You can drive there using Highway 4. It takes roughly two and a half hours to drive from Victoria.

Horne Lake Caves

British Columbia's Horne Lake Caves Provincial Park is a singular natural beauty. Visitors who wish to explore the intriguing underground world frequently visit this renowned location.

Things to Investigate:

- **Underground Wonders:** Discover a system of caverns with breathtaking crystal formations, rock formations, and prehistoric fossils.
- **Guided Tours**: Take a guided tour to discover more about the caverns' ecosystem, history, and geology.
- **Scenic Trails**: Take in the serene natural splendour while hiking through the nearby woodland.

Price:

- Guided tours are subject to admission fees. For the most recent prices, see the Horne Lake Caves website.

Scan the QR code
1. Open Camera: Launch your smartphone's camera app.
2. Position QR Code: Place the QR code within the camera's viewfinder.
3. Hold Steady: Keep the device steady for the camera to focus.
4. Wait for Scan: Wait for the code to be recognized.
5. Tap Notification: Follow the prompt to access the content.

How to Get There:

- On Vancouver Island, about 60 kilometres north of Nanaimo, is Horne Lake Caves Provincial Park. Highway 19 is the driving route to the park. To get to Horne Lake Caves, follow the signage.

MacMillan Provincial Park

On Vancouver Island, MacMillan Provincial Park, often known as Cathedral Grove, is a must-see location for those who enjoy the outdoors. Ancient Douglas fir trees, some of which are more than 800 years old and more than 80 metres tall, are its most well-known feature.

Things to Investigate:

- **Ancient Trees**: The chance to stroll among these imposing forest giants and be struck by their size and antiquity is the park's primary draw.
- **Scenic Trails**: The forest is home to a system of well-kept paths that provide chances for both easy walks and strenuous hikes.
- Numerous photo options are presented by the beautiful trees and tranquil woodland setting.

Price:

- Cathedral Grove is free to enter.

How to Get There:

- Cathedral Grove is roughly a two-and-a-half-hour drive from Victoria on Vancouver Island, off Highway 4.

Tofino

Two quaint seaside communities on Vancouver Island, Tofino and Ucluelet, are well-known for their breathtaking natural beauty, outdoor activities, and relaxed vibe.

Tofino

Things to Investigate:

- **Surfing**: With a variety of surf breaks suitable for surfers of all skill levels, Tofino is a top surfing destination.
- **Hiking**: Take paths like the Rainforest Trail and the Wild Pacific Trail to explore the untamed shoreline and magnificent woods.
- **Whale Watching**: To observe magnificent animals like humpback whales and orcas, take a whale-watching tour.
- **Kayaking**: Explore undiscovered coves and marine life as you paddle across calm coastal seas.
- **Hot Springs**: Unwind and revitalise the naturally occurring geothermal hot spring at Hot Springs Cove.

The Ucluelet

Things to Investigate:

- **Ucluelet Aquarium**: This interactive aquarium teaches about ecosystems and marine life.
- Hike the Wild Pacific Trail, which offers breathtaking views of the coastline and chances to see wildlife.
- Beachcombing is the practice of exploring beaches in search of treasures such as sea glass and shells.
- **Kayaking**: Explore the open ocean or paddle across the serene waters of Ucluelet Harbor.

How to Get There:

- **By Car**: Highway 4, a picturesque drive down Vancouver Island's west coast, is the primary route to Tofino and Ucluelet.
- **By Ferry:** After travelling to Nanaimo by ferry from Vancouver, you can drive to Tofino and Ucluelet.
- **By Air**: Major cities in British Columbia offer flights to Tofino.

Price:

- Depending on your spending limit and the activities you select, a trip to Tofino and Ucluelet may cost different amounts. Budget-friendly and upscale alternatives are available for lodging, dining, and entertainment.

The Nanaimo

The dynamic city of Nanaimo, located on Vancouver Island's east coast, combines outdoor recreation, cultural attractions, and scenic beauty.

Things to Investigate:

- Discover the breathtaking beaches, hiking paths, and historic sites of Newcastle Island Marine Provincial Park.
- **The Bastion:** A mediaeval fort with sweeping views of the city and the harbour.
- Discover the history, culture, and natural environment of the city at the Nanaimo Museum.
- **Trails for Biking and Hiking:** Explore the stunning paths in and around Nanaimo, including the

well-travelled paths in the Englishman River Provincial Park.

- **Local Cuisine**: Savour delectable desserts from the renowned Nanaimo Bar, artisan beer, and fresh seafood.

How to Get There:

- **Ferry**: From Vancouver or other mainland locations, Nanaimo is conveniently reachable by ferry.
- **Car**: Highway 19, which traces the east coast of Vancouver Island, is the route that leads to Nanaimo.

Price:

- Depending on your spending limit and the activities you select, a trip to Nanaimo may cost different amounts. Budget-friendly and upscale alternatives are available for lodging, dining, and entertainment.

The Campbell River

The "Salmon Capital of the World" is Campbell River, a bustling seaside community on Vancouver Island. It provides breathtaking natural beauty, a welcoming community, and a wide variety of outdoor activities.

Things to Investigate:

- **Fishing for Salmon**: As the name implies, the Campbell River is a popular spot for salmon fishing, drawing fishermen from all over the world.
- **Elk Falls Provincial Park** is a stunning park with hiking paths, lush woodlands, and tumbling waterfalls.

- Popular winter sports including skiing, snowboarding, and snowshoeing are available at Mount Washington Alpine Resort.
- Hiking, camping, and discovering isolated lakes and rivers are all possible in the expansive wilderness area known as Strathcona Provincial Park.
- **Paddleboarding and Kayaking**: Discover the serene waters of Discovery Passage while observing marine life such as whales, seals, and sea lions.

How to Get There:

- **By Car**: Highway 19, which traces the east coast of Vancouver Island, provides access to Campbell River.
- **By Ferry**: You can drive to Campbell River after taking a ferry from Vancouver to Nanaimo.

Price:

- Depending on your spending limit and the activities you select, a trip to Campbell River may cost different amounts. Budget-friendly and upscale alternatives are available for lodging, dining, and entertainment.

Totem Poles by Duncan

The quaint settlement of Duncan on Vancouver Island is well known for its enormous totem pole collection. These stunning pieces of art, which are dispersed across the city, provide a window into the Coast Salish people's rich cultural legacy.

Things to Investigate:

- **Totem Pole Walk:** Explore the city's numerous totem poles by going on a self-led walking tour. Every pole conveys a different tale, frequently featuring historical events, family crests, and mythological characters.

- **Local Stores and Galleries**: Visit the neighbourhood stores and galleries that offer one-of-a-kind handcrafted goods, such as jewellery, artwork, and carvings of totem poles.
- **Natural Beauty**: Take advantage of the hiking, fishing, and kayaking options in the neighbouring parks and Lakeside, as well as the surrounding natural beauty.

Price:

- There is no charge to observe the totem poles. However, you might have to pay for lodging, meals, and transportation.

How to Get There:

- Duncan is reachable by vehicle or public transit and is situated on Vancouver Island. It's a well-liked destination for tourists touring the island.

Cowichan Valley

Situated on Vancouver Island, the Cowichan Valley is a gorgeous area known for its vibrant culture, quaint communities, and breathtaking natural beauty.

Things to Investigate:

- **Kinsol Trestle**: Hiking and photography enthusiasts frequent this striking wooden railway bridge.

- The Cowichan Valley Trail is a picturesque route that passes through small villages, farms, and forests.
- **Local Wineries**: Visit the numerous vineyards in the area, including Unsworth Vineyards and Averill Creek Vineyard, to sample award-winning wines.
- Cowichan Lake is a stunning lake that is ideal for boating, fishing, and swimming.
- **Charming Towns**: Discover the distinctive stores, restaurants, and art galleries in Duncan, Lake Cowichan, and Mill Bay.
- **Adventures in nature**: Take part in a range of outdoor pursuits, such as biking, hiking, kayaking, and birdwatching.

How to Get There:

- Driving to the Cowichan Valley is simple. You may drive down Highway 1 to get there, and it's on Vancouver Island.

Price:

- Your budget and the activities you select will determine how much a trip to the Cowichan Valley costs. Budget-friendly and upscale alternatives are available for lodging, dining, and entertainment.

Cowichan Lake

Lake Cowichan: A Calm Retreat

On Vancouver Island, the charming village of Lake Cowichan lies tucked away on the shores of the calm Cowichan Lake. With lots of chances for outdoor leisure and relaxation, it provides a peaceful haven from the bustle.

Things to Investigate:

- **Cowichan Lake**: Boating, fishing, kayaking, and swimming are among the water sports available at this gorgeous lake.
- **Cowichan River**: This river offers fishing, whitewater kayaking, and beautiful float trips.
- **Hiking Trails**: Take a hike along the Trans Canada Trail to discover the nearby mountains and forests.
- **Local Stores and Dining Options**: Explore charming stores, galleries, and eateries serving delectable regional fare.
- **Relaxation**: Take in the serene ambiance and stunning surroundings while unwinding at one of the many lakeside resorts or campers.

How to Get There:

- On Vancouver Island, Lake Cowichan is reachable by car. From Victoria or Nanaimo, it's a well-liked weekend or day vacation destination.

Price:

- Depending on your spending limit and the activities you select, a trip to Lake Cowichan may cost different amounts. Budget-friendly and upscale alternatives are available for lodging, dining, and entertainment.

Chapter 2. Action Items

Kayaking and surfing

With top-notch surfing and kayaking spots, Vancouver Island is a haven for lovers of water sports.

Surfing

Tofino

- **Where to Surf:** Tofino is well known for its reliable surf breaks that are appropriate for surfers of all skill levels. Long Beach, Cox Bay, and Chesterman Beach are well-known surfing locations.
- Tofino may be reached by car by Highway 4 or by ferry from Vancouver to Nanaimo, after which you can drive down the west coast of the island.

Cost: Depending on the supplier, surfboard instruction and rentals might range in price. Check out the rates at nearby surf shops.

Canoeing

The Ucluelet and Tofino:

- **Where to Kayak**: There are several kayaking options in Tofino and Ucluelet, ranging from serene harbour paddles to daring sea kayaking excursions.
- **How to Get There**: You can drive or take a boat to Tofino and Ucluelet.

Cost: The cost of guided tours and kayak rentals varies based on the tour's duration and the supplier.

Extra Advice:

- **Best Time to Go**: April through October are the ideal months for kayaking and surfing because of the warmer water and more reliable waves.
- **Wetsuit**: In the colder seas of Vancouver Island, a wetsuit is necessary for kayaking and surfing.
- Prioritise safety by always consulting tidal charts and weather reports before leaving. Be mindful of possible dangers and wear a life jacket.
- **Guided Tours**: If you're new to kayaking or surfing, think about going on a guided trip.
- **Local Surf Shops**: Schedule lessons, rent gear, and consult with local surf professionals.

Trekking

From casual walks along the coast to strenuous mountain hikes, Vancouver Island has a wide variety of hiking paths. These are a few well-liked trekking locations:

National Park Reserve near Pacific Rim

- The world-famous multi-day West Coast Trail is recognized for its breathtaking coastal views, difficult terrain, and untamed beauty.
- The Broken Group Islands are a kayaker's dream come true, with many trekking paths spread over the different islands that provide chances to discover pristine beaches, woodlands, and unusual geological formations.
- **Rainforest paths**: Take pleasure in the verdant rainforest paths, like the Rainforest Trail and the Wild

Pacific Trail, which provide a variety of species and stunning vistas.

Provincial Park Strathcona

- **Golden Hinde Trail**: A strenuous climb that leads to the summit of Golden Hinde and provides expansive views of the valleys and mountains around it.
- **The Mystery Lake Trail** is a moderate climb that leads to a lovely alpine lake with breathtaking mountain views.

The Alpine Resort at Mount Washington

- **Hiking Trails**: Discover the forests and alpine meadows that encircle Mount Washington. There are hiking trails suitable for hikers of all skill levels.

Other Places to Go Hiking

- The Galloping Goose Trail is a well-travelled rail route that connects Victoria and Sooke and provides breathtaking views of the surrounding countryside and the Salish Sea.
- A neighbourhood park with a number of pathways, Mount Douglas Park provides breathtaking views of Victoria and the surrounding landscape.

How to Get There:

- You must go to Vancouver Island to reach these trekking locations. You can fly to Victoria International Airport or take a ferry from Vancouver to the island. To get to particular hiking spots on the island, you can either rent a car or take public transit.

Price:

- **Park costs**: A few parks, like Strathcona Provincial Park and Pacific Rim National Park Reserve, have admission costs.
- **Transportation**: Ferry tickets, rental vehicle prices, and public transportation prices will differ.
- **Accommodations**: Costs for lodging vary based on location and amenities, and alternatives include hotels and camping.

Advice:

- **Permits** are necessary for certain trails, such as the West Coast Trail, and must be reserved in advance.
- **Safety**: Keep an eye out for shifting weather patterns, particularly in mountainous regions. Bring emergency supplies, suitable footwear, and clothing.
- **Wildlife**: Observe safety precautions and be mindful of wildlife, such as cougars and bears.
- **Local Knowledge**: For the most recent trail conditions and safety recommendations, check with ranger stations or local information centres.

Going camping

From peaceful forest settings to campgrounds by the seaside, Vancouver Island has a wide variety of camping options. Here are a few well-liked locations for camping:

National Park Reserve near Pacific Rim

- **Camping**: There are a number of camping alternatives available in the park, such as wilderness camping on the Broken Group Islands and beachside camping at Long Beach.
- **How to Get There**: Ferries and cars are both accessible.
- **Cost**: Reservations are advised at the busiest times, and there are camping costs.

Provincial Park Strathcona

- **Camping**: There are many campsites in the park, including those next to scenic rivers and lakes.
- **How to Get There**: You can drive there.
- **Cost**: Reservations are advised at the busiest times, and there are camping costs.

Rathtrevor Provincial Park's beach

- **Camping**: Enjoy breathtaking views of the ocean while camping on the beach in this well-known campground.
- **How to Get There**: You can drive there from Parksville.
- **Cost**: Reservations are advised at the busiest times, and there are camping costs.

Other Well-liked Camping Locations:

- The Englishman River Provincial Park provides campsites close to the river, which is ideal for kayaking and fishing.
- Little Qualicum Falls Provincial Park offers hiking paths and camping areas next to stunning waterfalls.

- Camping on the beach with breathtaking views of the ocean is available at French Beach Provincial Park.

Fishing

From freshwater fishing for trout and steelhead to saltwater fishing for salmon and halibut, Vancouver Island has a wide variety of fishing options. Here are a few well-liked locations for fishing:

Saltwater Fishing

- **Campbell River**: Often referred to as the "Salmon Capital of the World," the Campbell River provides fantastic chances to capture Chinook, Coho, and Sockeye salmon.
- World-class saltwater fishing is available at Tofino and Ucluelet, two coastal communities where visitors can catch halibut, lingcod, and a variety of rockfish.
- **Port Hardy**: This seaside resort in the north has great halibut, salmon, and other saltwater fishing.

Freshwater Fishing

- **Cowichan River**: This river is well known for its superb trout and steelhead fishing.
- **Campbell River**: Steelhead, trout, and salmon can all be caught in the Campbell River.
- **Lakes on Vancouver Island:** Fishing for trout, bass, and other freshwater species is possible in several lakes on Vancouver Island, including Cowichan Lake and Cameron Lake.

How to Get There:

- You can take a plane or ferry to Vancouver Island to get to these fishing spots. To get to particular fishing spots on the island, you can either rent a car or take public transit.

Price:

- The type of fishing, the location, and whether you decide to charter a boat or hire a fishing guide can all affect the price of fishing on Vancouver Island. Additionally, you might have to buy fishing permits and licences.

Observing whales

With chances to see magnificent animals like humpback whales, orcas, and gray whales, Vancouver Island is a top whale-watching location. Here are a few well-liked spots for whale watching:

Victoria

- **Where to Watch**: From Victoria's Inner Harbour, several tour companies provide whale-watching excursions.
- **How to Get There**: You may fly or take a ferry from Vancouver to Victoria.
- **Cost**: The cost of a whale-watching tour varies based on the tour operator and the length of the trip.

Ucluelet and Tofino

- **Where to Watch:** Whale-watching cruises are available from both Tofino and Ucluelet through several tour operators.

- **How to Get There**: You can drive or take a boat to Tofino and Ucluelet.
- **Cost**: The cost of a whale-watching tour varies bases on the tour operator and the length of the trip.

The Campbell River

- **Where to Watch**: During the spring and fall migration, Campbell River is a well-liked spot to see whales.
- **How to Get There**: You can drive or take a ferry to Campbell River.

Cost: The cost of a whale-watching tour varies based on the tour operator and the length of the trip.

Observing Bears

Observing bears on Vancouver Island

- There are exceptional chances to see bears in their natural environment on Vancouver Island. The main places to see bears are as follows:

Observing Black Bears

- **Ucluelet and Tofino**: During salmon runs, black bears are frequently sighted in these coastal regions. Bears fishing for salmon can be seen on guided boat cruises.
- **Campbell River**: This region is well known for seeing black bears, particularly in Elk Falls Provincial Park and along the Campbell River.

Grizzly Bear Observation

- **Great Bear Rainforest:** A sizable grizzly bear population can be found in this isolated area on British Columbia's central coast. The greatest opportunity to see these amazing animals in their native environment is through guided tours.
- A great spot to see grizzly bears is Knight Inlet, a fjord. Visitors can see bears fishing for salmon and interacting with their environment during guided boat or floatplane tours.

How to Get There:

- **Ucluelet and Tofino**: Reachable by ferry or automobile.
- **Campbell River**: Reachable by ferry or automobile.
- **Great Bear Rainforest**: Reachable by floatplane or boat from a number of coastal locales, including Bella Bella and Port Hardy.

Price:

- Tour operators, destinations, and tour length all affect the cost of guided tours.
- **Transportation**: Flights, auto rentals, and ferry tickets will cost different amounts.
- **Accommodations**: Costs for lodging vary according to location and amenities, and options range from camping to opulent resorts.

Chapter 3. Itinerary

A Week-Long Journey

From cultural exploration to outdoor adventures, Vancouver Island has a lot to offer. To get the most out of your trip, consider the following suggested one-week itinerary:

Day 1: Get to Victoria

- **Morning**: Check into your hotel after landing at Victoria International Airport.

- **Afternoon**: Take a walk through the ancient streets, explore the quaint Inner Harbour, and stop by the Royal BC Museum.

- **Evening**: Savour a delectable meal at a restaurant by the water while taking in the breathtaking sunset.

Day 2: Whale Watching and Butchart Gardens

- **Morning**: Take in the magnificent display of flower beauty at the world-famous Butchart Gardens.

- **Afternoon**: take a whale-watching excursion from the Inner Harbor, where you may look for humpback whales, orcas, and other marine creatures.

- **Evening**: Have a quiet meal at your hotel or unwind at a neighbourhood bar.

Day 3: National Park at Pacific Rim

- **Morning**: Drive to Tofino in the morning and settle into your lodging.

- **Afternoon**: take a guided surf instruction or explore the gorgeous Long Beach and Chesterman Beach beaches.

- **Evening**: Savour a seafood meal at a nearby eatery while taking in the ocean sunset.

Day 4: Hot Springs and Rainforest

- **Morning**: Take a hike along the Rainforest Trail or the Wild Pacific Trail through Pacific Rim National Park's verdant rainforests.

- **Afternoon**: Unwind and relax in the mineral-rich waters of the Natural Geothermal Hot Springs Cove.

- **Evening**: Savour a warm meal at a neighbourhood eatery or bar.

Day 5: Kayaking and Island Hopping

- **Morning**: Explore the Broken Group Islands, a breathtaking archipelago with immaculate beaches and a wealth of wildlife, on a kayaking trip.

- **Afternoon**: go to Ucluelet, a picturesque village, and check out its galleries and stores.

- **Evening**: Savour a seafood meal at a nearby eatery while taking in the ocean sunset.

Day 6: Coastal Drive and Nanaimo

- **Morning**: Travel to Nanaimo and tour the 19th-century fort known as the Bastion.

- **Afternoon**: take a beautiful drive along the coast, including stops at Qualicum Beach and Parksville, two little communities.

- **Evening**: Unwind at your hotel after a seafood meal at a nearby restaurant.

Day 7: Leaving

- **Morning**: gather your belongings and depart from your lodging.

- **Afternoon**: Take in a last supper at a neighbourhood restaurant or spend your final hours touring Victoria's marketplaces and stores.

- **Evening**: Depart from Victoria International Airport in the evening.

Chapter 4. Accommodations

Pacific Sands Beach Resort

Situated in Tofino, British Columbia, the Pacific Sands Beach Resort is an opulent seaside resort. It provides a range of lodging choices, from comfortable beach homes to apartments by the sea. The resort offers convenient access to the beach, a range of on-site amenities, and breathtaking views of the ocean.

Price:

- The season, kind of room, and extra facilities all affect how much it costs to stay at the Pacific Sands Beach Resort. For the most recent information on availability and cost, it is advised to visit their website.

How to Get There:

Tofino, on Vancouver Island's west coast, is home to the Pacific Sands Beach Resort. You can get there by automobile or ferry.

- **By Car:** Highway 4 provides beautiful coastal vistas as you travel to Tofino.
- **By Ferry**: You can drive to Tofino after taking a ferry from Vancouver to Nanaimo.

The Black Rock Oceanfront Resort

Situated in Ucluelet, British Columbia, the Black Rock Oceanfront Resort is an opulent seaside resort. It provides cozy lodgings, breathtaking views of the ocean, and a number of facilities, such as a restaurant, spa, and fitness centre.

Price:

- The season, kind of room, and extra facilities all affect how much it costs to stay at the Black Rock Oceanfront Resort. For up-to-date pricing and reservation details, it is advised to visit their website.

How to Get There:

On Vancouver Island's west coast, in Ucluelet, sits the Black Rock Oceanfront Resort. You can get there by automobile or ferry.

- **By Car**: Highway 4 provides beautiful coastal vistas as you travel to Ucluelet.
- **By Ferry**: You can drive to Ucluelet after taking a ferry from Vancouver to Nanaimo.

Best Western Plus Nanaimo Conference Centre

Nanaimo, British Columbia, is home to the Best Western Plus Nanaimo Conference Centre. Because of its handy location and cozy lodgings, it's a well-liked option for both business and pleasure travellers.

Price:

- The season, kind of accommodation, and extra facilities all affect how much it costs to stay at the Best Western Plus Nanaimo Conference Centre. For up-to-date pricing and reservation details, it is advised to visit their website.

How to Get There:

Nanaimo, British Columbia, is home to the Best Western Plus Nanaimo Conference Centre. You can get there by automobile or ferry.

- **By Car**: Highway 19, which follows Vancouver Island's east coast, is a good route to take if you want to travel to Nanaimo.
- **By Ferry**: From Vancouver, you can go to Nanaimo by ferry.

Chapter 5. Cuisine

Seafood

The fresh and varied seafood of Vancouver Island is well known. Here's an idea of how much some well-known seafood dishes cost:

- **Salmon**: A main dish of wild-caught sockeye or farmed Atlantic salmon will cost about $20 to $30.
- **Halibut**: This firm, white fish is frequently grilled or served with fish and chips. A main course can cost anything from $25 to $35.
- **Crab**: A local specialty, Dungeness crab can be highly costly. The price of a crab plate can range from $30 to $40.
- **Oysters**: The cost of fresh oysters varies according to their size and type, but they are a must-try. The price range for a dozen oysters is $20 to $40.
- Clams and mussels are shellfish that are frequently used in steamed pots, pasta meals, and seafood chowders. A seafood platter with clams and mussels may cost between $25 and $35, though prices can vary.

Please be aware that these are only estimates and that actual expenses may differ according to the particular restaurant, time of year, and state of the market.

Farm-to-table cooking

The Farmhouse Kitchen

A well-known farm-to-table eatery in Victoria, The Farmhouse Kitchen is renowned for its delectable cuisine and use of seasonal, fresh ingredients. You can anticipate paying a low fee for a fine dining experience, while the precise cost of a dinner may vary based on the particular foods selected.

The Common Loaf

A well-known bakery in Tofino, The Common Loaf is renowned for its fresh bread and delectable baked items. You may anticipate paying a fair price for baked products, sandwiches, and pastries, however exact costs may differ.

The Red Fish

A well-known seafood restaurant in Victoria, The Red Fish is renowned for its inventive recipes and use of fresh, locally sourced ingredients. You can anticipate paying a moderate to high price for a fine dining experience, while the precise cost of a dinner may vary based on the particular foods selected.

Chapter 6. Transportation

Accessing Vancouver Island and Victoria

Ferry

The main way to travel from the mainland to Vancouver Island is via BC Ferries. The main routes and terminals are as follows:

Main Roads:

- The most well-travelled route to Victoria and Vancouver Island is from Tsawwassen (Vancouver) to Swartz Bay (Victoria). Conveniently, Tsawwassen's ferry station is close to Vancouver International Airport.
- Travelling from Tsawwassen (Vancouver) to Duke Point (Nanaimo) is the best way to see Nanaimo, Campbell River, and Port Alberni, as well as the eastern portion of Vancouver Island.
- The ferry voyage from Horseshoe Bay (West Vancouver) to Departure Bay (Nanaimo) is picturesque and offers breathtaking views of the coastline.

Price:

The route, size of the vehicle, and number of passengers all affect ferry ticket prices. For the most recent details on prices and reservations, it is advised to visit the BC Ferries website. Seniors, students, and locals frequently qualify for discounts.

Aircraft

Vancouver Island's main airport is Victoria International Airport (YYJ). Major Canadian cities including Vancouver, Calgary, and Toronto are among those that offer flights to it.

Victoria's Main Airlines:

- **WestJet**: Provides regular flights from major cities in Canada.
- Direct flights are offered by Air Canada from Vancouver and other places.
- British Columbian regional flights are provided by Pacific Coastal Airlines.

Price:

The airline, the dates of travel, and the time of booking all affect flight prices. To compare costs and locate the best offers, it is advised to utilise a travel booking website or app.

Automobile

Ferries are the only way to get to Vancouver Island by car. Below is a summary of the main route:

Path:

Get to a Ferry Terminal by Car:

- The most popular departure location is the Tsawwassen Ferry Terminal, which is close to Vancouver.
- The Horseshoe Bay Ferry Terminal is a picturesque route that is situated in West Vancouver.

Ferry Ride:

- The quickest way to get to Victoria is from Tsawwassen to Swartz Bay.
- Nanaimo, a significant city on Vancouver Island, may be reached via the Horseshoe Bay to Departure Bay route.

Price:

Driving to Vancouver Island costs the following:

- **Ferry Fare**: The size of your car, the number of passengers, and the season all affect how much the ferry ticket costs.
- **Fuel Costs**: The price of your car's gas.
- **Tolls**: There may be tolls, particularly if you're travelling across certain bridges or highways.

Moving About

Rent a Car

- **Car Rental:** The most practical method to see Vancouver Island is to rent a car. The Victoria International Airport (YYJ) and large cities like Nanaimo and Victoria are home to rental locations for major vehicle rental firms like Hertz, Avis, Budget, and Enterprise.
- **Cost**: The type of vehicle, the length of the rental, the season, and the rental business all affect the price of renting a car. To get the best bargain, it is advised to compare rates offered by several rental providers.

Driving On Vancouver Island:

- Beautiful coastline roads and picturesque drives can be found on Vancouver Island.
- **Highway 4:** With its stunning vistas of the Pacific Ocean, this roadway links Victoria with Tofino and Ucluelet.
- **Highway 19:** This road connects important communities like Nanaimo, Campbell River, and Port Hardy and travels along the island's eastern coast.

Public Transportation (Ferry, Bus)

Major communities like Victoria, Nanaimo, and Campbell River are served by BC Transit, the main public transportation company on Vancouver Island.

Terminals and Routes:

- Within these cities, BC Transit has a bus route network that connects to important locations like as
- **Ferry Terminals**: Nanaimo Harbour, Departure Bay, and Swartz Bay

Price:

Depending on the route and price class, riding BC Transit might cost different amounts. BC Transit provides a range of fare choices, such as:

- **Cash Fare**: Usually paid on the bus, this is a one-way fare.
- **DayPass**: A one-day pass that grants unrestricted movement within a certain area.
- A monthly pass that grants unrestricted travel within a certain area is known as a monthly pass.

Rental Bicycles

- City bikes, electric cycles, and mountain bikes are among the many types of bikes that Cycle BC rents out. They have handy sites in Nanaimo and Victoria.
- Road bikes, mountain bikes, and e-bikes are among the bikes available for rent at The Pedaler, a bike rental store in Victoria.
- **Oak Bay Bikes**: This Oak Bay-based store rents out a range of bikes, including e-bikes, road bikes, and mountain bikes.

Well-liked Cycling Paths:

- From Victoria to Sooke, the Galloping Goose path is a picturesque rail path that's ideal for a leisurely cycling ride.
- The Lochside Trail is a well-liked path that stretches along Victoria's waterfront and provides breathtaking harbour vistas.
- **Mount Douglas Park:** For more experienced mountain bikers, this park offers strenuous trails.
- **MacMillan Provincial Park**: Take a leisurely bike ride through Cathedral Grove's historic forests.

Enjoy beautiful coastal riding through the trees and along the beaches at Pacific Rim National Park.

The price of renting a bike:

- The type of bike, length of rental, and location all affect the cost of renting a bike. For a typical bike rental, you should budget between $20 and $40 per day. Renting an e-bike is usually more costly.

Ride-sharing and taxi services:

For your convenience, Vancouver Island has a number of ride-sharing and taxi options.

Large Cities:

- **Victoria**: In Victoria, both conventional taxi services and ride-sharing applications such as Uber and Lyft are easily accessible.
- **Nanaimo**: There are taxis and ride-sharing services in Nanaimo, particularly in the downtown and ferry terminal areas.
- **Tofino and Ucluelet**: Although there are taxis available, there may not be as many possibilities for ride-sharing.

Price:

- A number of variables, including distance, traffic, time of day, and any surge pricing, might affect the price of a taxi or ride-sharing service. To obtain real-time fare estimations, ride-sharing applications are advised.

Appendix: Resources

Contact details and helpful websites

Contact details and helpful websites for visitors to Vancouver Island

Vancouver Island tourism:

- https://vancouverisland.travel/ is the website.

This website offers a wealth of information about Vancouver Island, covering local events, lodging options, transportation, and attractions.

Ferries in British Columbia:

- https://www.bcferries.com/ is the website.

- 1-888-BC FERRIES (1-888-223-3779) is the contact number.
- The principal ferry company that links Vancouver Island with the mainland is BC Ferries. Ferry ticket booking, timetable checking, and route and terminal information are all available.

British Columbia tourism:

- https://www.hellobc.com/ is the website.

- This website offers general information on British Columbia, such as emergency contacts, travel advice, and weather forecasts.

Parks Canada:

- Pacific Rim National Park Reserve and Fort Rodd Hill National Historic Site are two of the numerous national parks and historic sites on Vancouver Island that are under the management of Parks Canada.

Parks in British Columbia:

- https://www.bcparks.ca/ is the website.

- Strathcona Provincial Park and MacMillan Provincial Park are two of the provincial parks on Vancouver Island that are overseen by BC Parks.

Emergency Services:

- **911**: The police, fire, and ambulance emergency number.

Extra Advice:

- **Weather:** Prior to your journey, review the forecast and be ready for a range of weather conditions, particularly along the coast.
- **Wildlife**: Pay attention to wildlife, particularly cougars and bears, and observe safety precautions.
- **First Aid Kit:** Bring a first aid kit in case of small wounds.
- **Local Information:** For more detailed information and suggestions, visit the visitor centres in your area.

Bonus: Photography Tips

Magic of the Golden Hour:

- **Early Morning**: As the sun rises over the mountains or water, capture the gentle, warm light.
- **Late Afternoon**: Dramatic lighting and beautiful silhouettes are produced by the golden hour.

Accept the Factors:

- **Foggy Mornings:** Photographs of misty landscapes often seem more ethereal and intriguing.
- **Rainy Days**: To capture distinctive reflections and melancholy ambiances, use umbrellas or rain covers for your camera.

Record the Specifics:

- **Close-ups:** Pay attention to the minute details found in nature, including the delicate beauty of flowers, the patterns of leaves, or the textures of bark.
- Discover the microscopic world of fungi, insects, and other tiny organisms through macro photography.

Make Use of Leading Lines

- **Natural Lines**: To direct the viewer's eye through the picture, use natural features like roads, rivers, or tree lines.
- Emphasise the architectural lines of bridges, buildings, and other man-made constructions.

Experiment with Various Viewpoints:

- **Bird's-Eye View:** Take pictures of expansive areas from above.
- **Worm's-Eye View:** To highlight height and scale, experiment with low-angle photographs.

- **Unusual Viewpoints:** To give your photographs a new viewpoint, experiment with unusual angles.

Utilise Light and Shadow to Your Advantage:

- **Backlighting**: Produce spectacular backlighting effects and silhouettes with the sun.
- **Side Lighting**: Use side lighting to draw attention to features and textures.
- **Front Lighting**: For landscapes and portraits, use a gentle, uniform light.

Take Local Culture Into Account:

- **People and Places**: Document the locals, their customs, and Vancouver Island's distinct culture.
- **Street photography**: Capture unscripted moments and daily life in places like Victoria and Nanaimo.

For stability, use a tripod:

- **Long Exposures**: Use them to catch the motion of stars in the night sky or to create smooth water effects.
- **Low-Light Photography**: Enhance the quality of your photos in low light.

Modify Your Images:

- **Basic Editing**: To improve your photos, change the exposure, contrast, and white balance.
- **Creative Editing**: To produce original and artistic images, play around with filters, effects, and cropping.

Author's Note

A Sincere Request for Your Evaluation

My goal as a travel writer is to encourage and mentor other adventures. In order to give you the best tour to Victoria and Vancouver Island, I put my all into writing this book, utilizing both my personal experiences and a great deal of research.

Your complimentary review and comments are really helpful to me. They assist other travelers in making well-informed judgments regarding their own travels in addition to validating my efforts. You can support a community of travellers who are passionate about exploration and discovery by sharing your experiences and insights.

I spent a lot of time and money discovering Victoria and Vancouver Island's splendor. In addition to motivating me to keep producing top-notch travel articles, your review will encourage other budding travel writers to follow their dreams.

I appreciate you reading my book and taking the time to comment. I am so grateful for your support.

Made in the USA
Columbia, SC
16 December 2024

49398470R00043

BOB, JIM, HEAVEN AND HELL

Eric Gurr

*What happens when we die and what can we learn from those
who have come back?*

ISBN: 978-1-7200-1906-0

AUTHOR'S PREFACE

Stories of near death experiences, or NDEs have been recorded for thousands of years. In Plato's Republic there is a story of a soldier who had died, gone to Heaven and returned. That soldier reported seeing "delights and visions of a beauty beyond words." The soldier was told that he would return and be a messenger to Earth of this other world. Another account from 1791 by Rear Admiral Sir Francis Beaufort[1] tells of an experience he had while nearly drowning in which he had a life review and "a calm felling of the most perfect tranquility." Similar to so many of the more current NDEs Beaufort also mentions that time was difficult to discern.

A case from Alexander Ogsten in 1919 tells of an out of body experience where he saw another patient in a different part of the hospital who had died. Similar to more modern stories of NDEs this observation of Ogsten's was verified by Nuns after the incident.[2]

These are just a very small sample of the thousands of near death experiences I catalogued and analyzed to write the fictional account of the experiences of Bob Fisher and Jim Stahlhaber. They show an amazing consistency over thousands of experiences. While the story is fictional, every experience in the first few chapters happened. There were many stories with much more detail but if they were not repeated I did not include them as part of Bob or Jim's near death experiences.

I am a data analyst by trade. I work with companies that sell products all over the world. I pull data out of a databases and help these companies to analyze sales trends. Using that same methodology, I decided to do an analysis of these NDEs.

I was trying to find the answer to a few questions that I thought might be learned through this analysis.

- What is Heaven really like?
- What are we supposed to do here on Earth?
- How should we live our lives?
- And perhaps most importantly, why aren't we happier?

Rather than compile all of this data into a boring report I decided a better approach would be to present the data in the form of a novel. It is a work of fiction and all of the characters are made up and exist only in my mind and on the pages of this book.

For the experience of the afterlife itself, I only used information that was produced by more than a few people. There is much that was new to me and I thought very interesting.

Regarding experiences with the afterlife, some who are very religious and have a near death experience are no longer religious and think it unimportant after. While others who are atheists, agnostics or not religious at all become very religious

For those who would suggest we must employ the scientific method and absolute rigors of science to come to any conclusions we are going to have a problem. The scientific method works great for our physical universe. But these experiences take place outside the normal physical dimensions of our world. Our scientific investigation ends at the narrative. We don't know how to cross the barrier into other dimensions.

The last problem however is the most significant. If the agnostics says, "There may be a God but I see no evidence of that." He is in conflict with himself and thus has no premise for a logical response. IF you acknowledge that there could be a creator with intelligence behind the universe, surely that intelligence would be great enough to conceal the method of creation or his location.

The question I often get in response to this is,

"Why would God want to hide from us?"

I don't think God is hiding. I also don't believe that God would come down to our humble little planet and walk around and tell us how to live. If God created us with free will the last thing he would do is magically appear out of the sky every day and frighten us into submission. It makes no sense. If God created the entire universe he certainly could have created humans that did exactly what he wanted them to do. Instead he gave us free will, love, and emotions.

Over the past few decades many books have been written about these NDEs. The vast majority of these books tell the story of an experience of one person. Beyond these books there are websites and other compilations of thousands of these experiences.

The experiences are real. They are things that have happened multiple times in this data. The instances of bright, beautiful lights are very common. Some people report going through a tunnel, while others say that the light came upon them and moved towards them. Still others say that it is more of a curtain or veil being lifted as opposed going through a tunnel. In these instances where there are similarities but no clear consensus I just picked one and ran with it.

Another problem I ran in to time and time again, is that people would report a very specific thing, but describe it differently.

One example is a tree. Many people report seeing a huge tree in the middle of a field. Some just mention the tree in passing. Others are very detailed and say that this tree has many different types of leaves with very brilliant colors. Still other experiences say nothing at all about a tree.

This is the nature of data analysis of stories or text. So to analyze these aspects of the data I assign meta-data to the object or experience. This type of analysis is often referred to as data science. But that's not really true. If I ascribe the term "tree" as meta-data and then aggregate all

of those stories with a tree in them it just raises more questions and presents more diversity of the data.

So I add another meta-data point. Now I have 'trees' and 'bright colors'. As you can probably surmise I've now eliminate those who saw a tree but didn't comment on the color! My meta-data now becomes too important and begins to skew my analysis. When this problem came up in my research I did what I do in my job as a data analyst. I look at the data in its entirety and say, "With what I have, this is about the best explanation I can give for the situation." Thus I can build a logical case for trees, or any other aspect that is hard to quantify as important to the experience.

There are other nuggets of information that are very rare but so profound I decided to include them. One of the most fascinating was the nature of logic in Heaven. There are several mentions of this in the experiences I researched, but not enough to quantify a clear definition. So I went with what I could best surmise.

I did this not because it was in any way important. I just found it interesting that a few individuals said there was no need for logic. Not that what they learned was illogical. What they articulated was that they understood everything about life, the universe and God that they didn't need any logic to explain it. They just knew everything perfectly.

I am not an ordained minister or priest. Some may disagree with my conclusions or suggest that they are not scripture. I get that. I really can't argue the point. All that I can say is that the evidence is compelling. I hope that this disagreement doesn't detract from the research, the enjoyment of the story or the impact it may have on your life.

CONTENTS

7

BOB'S LIFE RIGHT NOW

I just don't... I can't stand this Tom. I want to know now. For the last few years I've felt like my life is just ripping apart at the seams."

Tom stared at Bob with a soft smile and responded.

"They'll tell us today or at worst Monday. It makes for a long weekend but we'll know soon enough. If it's not me I hope it's you. I really mean that."

"Thanks Tom. It's just, I just need this. It's been a rough few years you know? I feel like my life is rattling apart. I mean, I thought I was on a great path and then when the bottom fell out back in 2008 I figured I'd bounce back a little quicker than I did. But I didn't.

Then things began to get worse. I probably spent more money than I should have and saved less but you get in these habits. It's so easy to go buy a new car, new carpet, granite for the kitchen and stainless steel appliances. I racked up a fortune in credit cards even when I was pulling in two hundred and fifty a year. Ya' know?

Life isn't supposed to be like this is it? We did all the right things didn't we? Went to college and worked hard."

Bob stopped and took a deep breath. Embarrassed for himself he looked at Tom. He paused for a moment trying to collect his thoughts. He shouldn't have gone off on a rant. He felt stupid.

If Tom Lawson was to get the promotion he would be Bob's new boss. And he had just unloaded all of his personal problems on the man.

"I'm sorry Tom. I'm making too big a deal out of this. I guess I got impatient for some reason. Sorry bud."

Tom just smiled back.

"It'll be fine Bob. You've got a great reputation here. Heck they talk about you all the time. You are the go getter. You really have nothing to worry about. You're great at your job and they really like you here."

"Yeah I know Tom. Hey and if you get the spot, I'll get the next one that opens up."

With that Tom smiled softly and walked out of Bob's office.

Bob wondered why he had never connected with Tom. Tom Lawson was by all appearances a great guy. He was always friendly and genuine and always smiling. He was just a little too religious for Bob's tastes. He had never been preachy but Bob kept his distance just to be safe. He was pretty certain that the executive management team wasn't exactly the church type.

Tom was one of those guys that could kill a good time at the bar after work. He didn't go with them all that much and drank iced tea or maybe a glass of wine. The other guys in the office drank to have fun. Tom was never judgmental, and he always left after just a drink or two. He was just one of those guys that for some reason made you feel like you were doing something wrong.

Bob pinched the bridge of his nose between his thumb and his fore finger. The action pushed his glasses up awkwardly. He brushed back his

hair with his fingers and was reminded that he needed another haircut. It was always something. If he didn't get a haircut the grey would come out. If he kept it just the right length the grey would blend perfectly with the brown at his temples. It made him look seasoned, but not old. He wasn't even forty and when his hair got too long the grey came out everywhere.

It used to be so easy. When money was easy, life was easy. Ten years ago he was on top of the world. Only in his mid-twenties he and his wife had bought a home that they could barely afford. They had two young daughters and another child on the way.

He spent money like there was no tomorrow. He knew it didn't matter. He was sure of it. Tomorrow he would just make more money. They had gone on lavish vacations and spent money on designer purses and shoes. If it was new and perceived as better or a luxury brand, they had to have it.

Bob Fisher was on a hamster wheel spinning at a hundred miles an hour and the stuff they bought was his scorecard. The more stuff and the more expensive the stuff the better Bob thought they were doing. His plan was to start saving for retirement when he hit his early forties. Save a hundred thousand dollars a year for ten years then retire early.

Then it had all fallen apart. The job was gone. The twenty thousand dollar commission checks five or six times every year and the big year-end bonus were all gone.

It had been really bad for a few years. But over the last few months he started to notice that he wasn't quite as stressed as he had been when he was making big money. He was spending more time with Donna and the kids. He also noticed that time spent with them was actually more fun. He was wearing older shoes and had even bought a few shirts off of a clearance rack. Had it really affected his life that much?

He also noticed that he felt physically better. The rat race had taken a toll on his body. He shouldn't have had back aches in his mid-thirties. He

shouldn't have been so tired all the time. But when he finally let a little of the stress go he felt better.

Something in the back of his mind hated that. He wanted to be the bigger than life provider for his family. He wanted to be seen as successful by people he would never see again. He wanted to complain about spending ten thousand dollars a year on horseback riding lessons. Some very big and deep part of Bob wanted to get back to where he was before. Something inside him hated the fact that he couldn't keep up with the Joneses.

He didn't want to keep up with the Joneses, he wanted to be the Joneses. He wanted to be the guy that people were trying to keep up with. To Bob there was nothing worse than being average. And he knew for certain that his wild spending had pushed him below average.

When he had finally landed this job he had worked like crazy. But it wasn't the same as it had been early in his career. He worked with a purpose. He wanted to understand everything he possibly could about the motors that his company sold. He wanted to understand everything he could about his customers and potential customers.

He worked hard and smart. He put in his time and made sure he got noticed by upper management. In early and out late.

But in the last year he had fallen slowly back in to those old habits. He was moving towards success and didn't feel he had to work so hard. Then when word of a retirement and new promotion had popped up he had buckled down again. He was the top producer in the company for the last two months. But he knew something was missing. He had to impress the bosses. He had to get his confidence and swagger back.

There was no logic to any of it. He shook his head and laughed at himself.

In many ways his life had improved. Whatever the reason he had to admit his life in almost every aspect, other than money, was much better.

Yet the stress was still there. There were still too many times when he couldn't buy the things he wanted. He was only taking care of the things he needed. He was trying to fill something missing in his life. He knew that now. But what was missing?

He laughed to himself at the thought of his little girls playing soccer at school. Just sitting there and watching them had been so much fun. And it was so much cheaper than tennis at the club and swimming lessons. But somehow it was so much more fun.

Then he thought about when he and Donna tried to learn how to cook. They had never had to do that. So many times they had tried some new recipe on the cheap. They ended having to force it down or throw it away a few too many times. But it had been so much fun.

"No!" He screamed inside his head.

"Don't become complacent. Having a lot of money is better. I'll find time for Donna and the kids. This is about me!" Sometimes the best way to help your family is to be a little selfish. He had to put the thoughts out of his head. He was the killer. He was the go getter. He was the man who got stuff done and he was going to get paid for it. He wanted to the old life back and he was going to get it. He wanted it to change.

Change was coming. Bob's life would change today but that had more to do with Tony Tripp than it did the promotion. Bob had no idea who Tony Tripp was. Tony Tripp had no idea who Bob Fisher was and the two would never meet. But Tony was about to affect Bob's life in a way neither could comprehend.

Tony smoked a little pot at lunch that day. It wasn't the first time. But today maybe he had smoked a little too much. Had he been paying more attention he would have tightened the oil plug in the truck he was working on. If had done that all of the oil wouldn't have leaked out on route 122 at that dangerous bend. That oil would mix with a very light rain. Just enough of a rain where you had to turn your windshield wipers on for

a minute or two. Bob would be driving his old Corvette in just a few hours along the same route as the truck with the oil leak.

And that little bit of oil on the road would lead to more changes than Bob could have ever imagined.

BOB FISHER DIES

I t was close to the end of the day. The executive team had finally gotten around to calling him into the conference room. Why did they always do this so late on a Friday? All week he had been waiting for this and now they finally call him in at 3:00 in the afternoon.

Roger Davidson, The VP of sales was talking and Bob was struggling to listen.

"It really came down to you and Tom Lawson." He said.

"And the reality is that Tom's numbers are a bit better than yours over the last year and he has a few more years with the firm."

Bob wondered if the two men could see his face drop. He felt as if his dog had just died and someone had punched him in the stomach at the exact moment. He knew his numbers were better than Tom's the last two months. Really they were a lot better. But he also knew that much of the reason was Tom's sales had fallen just a bit while with all of his hard work Bob's sales had only reason slightly. He was certain he had lost the promotion, but the man kept talking.

"I don't want you to get me wrong here Bob, Tom is also a great guy. I mean we really like him. But he is just a little too churchy for us. Do you know what I mean?"

He winked and smiled at Bob as he said it. Bob smiled back nodding that he understood completely.

"We like you Bob. You're a real killer. We think you are the man for the job. You fit in culturally with the rest of the leadership team and we

think you hold the same values that we do. You've got a bright future in this company. We feel lucky to have you and we firmly believe this promotion is just the first of many. We'll have your stuff moved in to the corner office Monday morning and we'll get your company car and salary and bonus plan all figured out by the end of next week."

Bob felt a wave of relief. It went from the top of his head to the bottom of his feet. He was trying to contain his excitement. He needed to act like he expected this and deserved it. He had to keep that professionalism at the highest levels. He was struggling with just the right words of acknowledgement, confidence and ease. He wanted them to know he appreciated it, but at the same time he expected it and deserved it.

But the words, the line of bull that used to come so easily to him would not come. So he just sat there with a dumb smile on his face nodding. Thankfully the awkward silence was broken. And the next words from Davidson, the VP almost put him over the edge.

"And Bob, I'm not getting any younger. We really want you to be here for the rest of your career. I'd like to start setting aside half a day a week to mentor you and show you what I do. Not a promise Bob, not gonna let you take my job tomorrow!"

Davidson laughed and Bob joined in like it was the funniest thing he had ever heard. He was finally able to squeak out a few words, "

Well Roger, I'm sure I've got a lot to learn still."

David McCarron, the president of the company finally spoke. "Rog, you keep telling me how smart and aggressive Bob here is. If he's as quick a study as you say, maybe he could take your job tomorrow."

And now all three men were laughing at how funny and clever they all were.

"But seriously Bob, we really think you might be able to handle that pretty quickly. If I can get you up to speed with some of the bigger accounts

I'd really like to retire soon. You should really plan on prepping your own replacement within the next year. Sound good?"

Bob was in a daze. He just smiled and nodded. "Sounds great Roger."

With that the men all stood up and shook hands with Bob and made small talk. But Bob was having trouble focusing. He had gotten the promotion and a million things were going through his mind. How soon would he actually be VP? When would he get the new car? How fast would the raise show up on his pay check?

He knew today would be a great day. But it had gotten so much better. VP was something that was just so far away. He just wanted to get back on his feet. To get back to where he was and if lucky, maybe a little further ahead. But now? Now everything was possible. Roger Davidson was loaded. The guy had to be pulling in well over half a million per year in salary alone. He could retire in a year and Bob would be a Vice President of the entire sales operation!

For the rest of the day he found it hard to focus. Twice Jim Stahlhaber had called. That was one customer Bob was glad he wouldn't have to deal with as much. Bob hated Stahlhaber so both times the phone rang he had sent him to voice mail. He knew he should be focusing on the tasks in front of him but he couldn't concentrate. He spent the last few minutes of the afternoon walking around making small talk and accepting the congratulations from his coworkers.

Most of the guys had been jealous. Bob could sense it. The congratulations and back slapping was nothing more than kissing up. Tom Lawson had been the only one to seem honestly happy for Bob. He wondered if Tom knew that he would soon be VP and was just better at sucking up than the rest of the guys. The thought made him cringe for some reason he couldn't quite put his finger on. The day ended in a blur.

He was back on top. He was driving home from work and already thinking about buying a new BMW, hell maybe even a Mercedes if the

company was paying for it why not? After the last few years of struggle he deserved a bit of luxury back in his life.

Donna could quit work. They could buy new clothes and furniture. They could buy all the things he wanted for the kids. The day had just been too crazy. In just another year or two he was going to make more money than he ever had. He wasn't going to catch up to his old life, he was going to exceed it.

He wouldn't have to drive the old Corvette every day and hope it didn't break down on him. He wouldn't have to stress about Donna driving his kids in an old van that could break down and leave them stranded. Life was about to get good again. And maybe really good.

At the back of his mind something was troubling him. He wasn't nearly as happy about the promotion as he should have been. And then it hit him. This was going to mean longer hours and travel. He would be away from the kids. And little Cameron was going to be eleven years old. She wasn't going to want to be around the family in a few years. He had to enjoy the time he had before she became a teenager.

Longer hours and more travel also meant less time with Donna. They had gotten so close over the last few years. When he hit the road he knew the temptations would follow. There were always single men and women at those conferences who would hang out at the bar at night. He knew a few married guys had cheated and gotten caught.

Five years ago he would have worried about getting caught because his wife would take half of his money. He tried to push that thought from his mind, but he knew it was true. Today he couldn't imagine hurting Donna like that.

Where were these thoughts coming from?

Bob was about making money. Big money. And with big money Donna and the kids would be fine. Actually he was making a great sacrifice!

He did enjoy time with the kids and with Donna. He loved watching them play soccer and helping Donna cook dinner.

With the money he was making now, and even more when he got the VP slot, he could hire a maid and really a part time cook. And they could eat out at nicer restaurants when he was out of town. They loved eating at nice places.

"How did life get so complicated?" He said out loud.

He smiled again. The sadness was confusing. This was a problem, but it was a good problem. He had no idea how to solve it. He knew there was something missing. Some crucial part of the equation that he couldn't put his finger on.

He shook his head trying to clear his brain. This was a great day. The best day he had had in a long time. He wanted to focus on enjoying the moment. He would figure out the rest later. Right now he just wanted to be happy for himself. He turned the radio on, put a smile on his face and set his mind determined to enjoy the rest of his ride home.

One of the nagging problems with the old Corvette was that it had no cup holders and no place for a cell phone. Bob got in the habit of putting his phone in the pocket under the dashboard just in front of the passenger seat.

As soon as he heard his familiar ring tone he cringed. He had forgotten to call Jim Stahlhaber back. When Stahlhaber called it always meant a problem. This was the third time the man had called and he knew he had to answer the phone. Bob prided himself on the fact that he could get along with anyone. But not Jim Stahlhaber. The guy was just a jerk.

He reluctantly reached across the seat to pick up the phone and answer it. Just as he was bringing it towards him the phone bumped the gear shift and fell to the floor. He tried to reach it but his seatbelt prevented him. He pressed the button and pulled the belt aside. As he

instinctively reached for his phone with his right hand his left hand naturally turned the steering wheel to the right.

Earlier that very afternoon a panel van had broken down at exactly the spot on the road that he was driving over now. The van stopped and oil leaked out forming a large puddle. The light rain that had just begun falling mixed with the oil and the road was slick.

The front wheels slid. The back wheels of the corvette slipped just for a second but then caught dry pavement

That little catch is what eventually caused his heart to stop beating. The car shot suddenly forward and sideways at the same time. At just over sixty miles per hour he hit the small bridge embankment with the left front of the car.

The explosive sound of crunching fiberglass, breaking glass and screeching metal were deafening.

His body flew forward and back so quickly that every muscle in his body instantly hurt. Now all was silent. The pain in his chest was dull. He knew he'd have a bruise and blood from a cut on his forehead was slowly dripping into his left eye. He lay with his head on the passenger seat and attempted to assess the situation.

He tried reach his phone to call 911 but a sharp pain shot up his leg. He managed to tilt his head down just enough to see that his left ankle was clearly broken.

The sudden motion of his body being slammed around the inside of his car nauseated him. He wanted to get out of the car so he could vomit. But he could not move. He couldn't figure out if the pain was holding him in place or if he was actually trapped.

The steering wheel had pressed against his chest and into his heart at impact, causing a slight tear in his aorta. He just laid still.

The silence was interrupted by a slamming car door. He was starting to feel light-headed when an older man shouted at him through the broken glass in the driver's side door.

"Hey buddy! Are you ok?"

Bob turned slightly and tried to speak. "I think I'm ok but my left foot is broken and my chest hurts pretty badly. Can you call 911 for me?"

He slipped out of consciousness and then woke up a few minutes later in the back of an ambulance. He tried to clear his mind but couldn't focus on anything. He still felt like he was going to be sick. He could feel the moisture in his mouth increasing and he was sweating profusely. He started to slowly rock from side to side and heard himself moaning.

He caught a glimpse of the blue shirt the EMT was wearing. Something wasn't right. He could feel it. They were working on him and that gave him slight comfort. But the look of concern on their faces worried him. Soon he would be in the hospital.

He thought just seconds had passed when he opened his eyes again but he was now lying on a bed in the hospital. He looked up at a woman who was working over him. The doctor saw his eyes and tried to muster a smile but Bob could see the frustration, or was it fear, in her eyes. She patted the side of his arm.

"We're going to get you all patched up Mr. Fisher. And your wife is on the way. We've given you something for the pain. Is it starting to feel better?" She asked.

Bob tried to smile and nodded.

"Okay that's great. You're going to be fine."

He was not. The leak in his aorta was starving his heart of blood and he went into cardiac arrest. He heard the beeping of the instruments and saw the doctors and nurses rushing around in a controlled panic. The

female doctor was shouting orders to those around her. Bob's eyes were open and trying to track her movements and listen to figure out what was going on. The doctor bent over him very close to his face just as his eyes were closing.

"Bob! Bob stay with us! Stay with us Bob we need you to fight with us!"

He tried to look up at the doctor. It was difficult to keep his eyes open and the light just above him caused him to squint. He felt his eyes closing and could no long struggle to even concentrate on keeping them open.

And then he was outside of his body. He was above the room floating near the ceiling.

Bob was fully conscious and aware. He felt no pain. He felt no emotion of any kind at all. He was dead and he knew it. His reaction to this was simply matter of fact. He felt no sadness of any kind. He was completely accepting of the situation.

Looking down from near the ceiling he could still see the doctors and technicians working on him. There were lights and other medical devices over his body but they were somehow transparent. He could see right through them. He noticed that only the people were not transparent.

A nurse had ripped off his shirt and the doctor was cutting into his chest. Another nurse was drawing blood. He could clearly see the scalpel slicing into him but he felt no pain and no anxiety about seeing this.

He felt no differently than if it had been his car being worked on. His body was simply the vehicle he used to transport himself around the earth.

He realized that he could see outside of the room. He could see that there were walls, but he could see through them. There were people

walking in the hallways. At the end of a long hallway leading out of the hospital he saw his wife.

Donna was running alongside an orderly with tears streaming down her face. He was able to move down directly in front of her. He could hear her crying. He wanted to tell her that he was okay. But she could not see him. She walked right past him as if he wasn't there.

He turned to look back to his room but there were several other rooms along the hallway that he could see.

In one of the rooms a little girl, probably five or six years old was laying in her bed laughing as her dad read her a story. In the room next to the little girl a very old man was laying on the table. His family was beside him. His wife was holding the man's hand and crying. The others around the man, his children looked sad but resigned. The man's breathing was so incredibly slow.

When the man took his last breath the nurse standing off to the side quickly rushed in and announced time of death. She looked at the family and said, 'He's gone now.' All of the family broke out in loud sobs and crying.

Bob saw the man leave his body. The man became visibly younger every second that he moved away from his body. He lingered for a second to look at his family. And even though they were crying and sad, the content smile never left the man's face. He looked directly back at Bob, the smile still on his face, quickly rose and disappeared.

Bob made his way back to his own room and looked down again at his own body. The doctor was yelling at the nurse.

"Let's go, let's go, let's go! We need to get that bleeding stopped or we're going to lose him. Hustle people hustle."

Bob felt the frustration of the doctors and nurses and the technicians. He wanted to tell them that this was not important and that

they should just relax. He felt strange that they were so worried about his body.

It was just his body, it wasn't him. He knew this perfectly and felt repulsed that the people were so worried. His body had nothing to do with him, why were they so upset?

He looked outside the hospital building to the parking lot. He could see people getting out of their cars and walking hurriedly towards the doors. He saw a field across the street with weeds and wild flowers growing in it and decided he wanted to go see that field. But he was being slowed down. He felt a hand on his back, or some kind of presence next to him guiding him upwards.

For a just a few seconds all went black. He knew his eyes were open and he could see but everything was black. He noticed with a passing curiosity that the walls had substance. The black was not a void. The walls were made of velvet or something very similar. He reached out his hand and found that he could touch them.

There was nothing to see but there was something there.

A tiny gold point of light appeared in the distance. It was a color of gold he had never seen before. Gold but with a hint of sky blue. He began moving rapidly towards the light and it grew. All around him were tiny but very bright stars racing past.

He sensed that he was moving away for earth through the universe and that these stars were the same stars he could see in the sky on a very clear night.

Another thought quickly took over. He thought that these weren't stars at all but people. Some kind of intelligence was behind the stars, or inside them. He wondered if those specks of light could see him as a star moving through space as well. He could not help but try to figure out how fast he was moving and how far away the single golden light was. He was

certain that he was far from the hospital. But was he really moving across the universe?

The light grew brighter. The tiny little speck of gold-blue was growing in size and intensity. The blackness around him was lifting and the other lights were fading. He could not process what was happening but it caused him no stress or concern at all. He could see both in front of him and behind him at the same time. He had a three-hundred and sixty degree view and he could see it and process it clearly.

A warmth was coming. He could feel it as if he had a body. And yet he knew he did not. He was just Bob Fisher, the soul and spirit. His body was nothing but a vapor and his consciousness. But he felt the warmth. It was growing and embracing him.

The warmth became a feeling of love deeper than he had ever experienced. He was in awe. Everything felt absolutely perfect.

As the blackness disappeared he was fully embraced by the brilliant light. It was brighter than the sun yet it did not hurt his eyes or cause him to squint like the light in the hospital had. The gold of the light was now gone and it was a soft blue. It was the warm blue of a completely clear September sky.

Standing before him was a group of people. Perhaps seven or eight but maybe ten or twelve he could not be sure because they were standing close to each other and they were blurry.

He could not make out their faces or much more than a silhouette of a body on each one. They were clustered close together. The people were gold in color. A soft fuzzy gold but at the same time stunningly beautiful.

His first thought was that he loved these people. He loved them more than anyone he had ever loved or thought he could love. They did not speak to him. They did not smile or frown at him. But Bob was smiling as

he felt he must have smiled as a small child when his parents returned from being away for some time.

He had heard stories of people dying and coming back to life and saying they felt an awesome love. But this was not well explained. He understood clearly now that it was not he who was loved by the people in front of him.

Perhaps they did but he didn't really consider it. What he knew for certain was that He loved them. He didn't care if they loved him or not. It made no difference. He wanted to be right here standing in front of them for eternity. He was a thirty-eight year old man and he wanted to jump up and down for joy. He wanted to skip, smile and laugh.

The love he felt was something that jarred his entire soul. This was the definition of bliss. This was pure love and pure happiness. He could actually feel love in the cells of his body.

Love was not some ethereal feeling or abstract concept. Love was a physical thing as real as the ground he had been standing on just a few hours before.

He thought briefly of the love he felt for Donna and his children and parents. He thought of that love as a two way bond between him and them. This love was different. He understood it completely. This love was not two way it was infinite ways. It was the power of love you feel for your children multiplied so many times that it could never be counted. It was truly infinite.

He wanted this to be forever. This feeling of love. He knew instinctively that he was home. This is where he was supposed to be. He thought that he understood clearly why the universe was so big. It had to be to hold all of this love. And yet it wasn't nearly big enough. The love was bursting the very walls of the universe. And this place so filled with love was his real home.

It bothered him not at all that this was not what he thought Heaven would be like. To him this was absolute perfection. Just to stand and love these people, or angels, or spirits or whatever they were, he could not decide and did not care.

After a short time, he could not tell how long, of just standing and smiling he could constrain himself no longer. He jumped two times out of pure joy and then started to run towards them. As he got closer he could make out smiles on their faces. They were not the same type of smile that Bob had. These were soft, very content smiles. He tried to run faster but could not reach them.

When he was very close they parted down the middle and faded away. Then the darkness behind them lifted and he could see another golden light. The light was the same color of gold as the people who had faded away but much brighter.

Out of the light another group of people began to walk towards him. As their faces became clear Bob fell to his knees and began to softly weep. He covered his face with his hands for just a second. He looked again at the man at the front of the group. It was his father.

He sprang to his feet and ran to him. He then recognized some of the other people. His grandmother, an aunt who had passed years ago and a cousin who had died very young. Some were familiar to him but he didn't know quite who they were.

He stopped in front of his father. He had died just a few years ago and Bob thought of him every day. His father didn't look as he had remembered. He was much younger. His appearance reminded Bob of a picture he had seen of his father many times. His wedding picture. He not only looked the same age he had the same look of happiness to him.

"Hello Bobby" His father said. Or at least all that Bob could understand. He heard his father's voice clear, loud and perfect. But his mouth did not move. He felt that his father was trying to tell him

something but he couldn't understand. The others around him started moving away. And quite quickly his father was gone as well. Bob tried to follow but he was stuck. He was alone but somehow he was not. He could still feel the love. For a moment he was content just to stand and feel. But it didn't last.

BOB SEES ANGELS AND HEAVEN

Bob was moving again. He was moving within the light. He could hear a slight humming. It started out as a buzzing but then became musical. As he was moving he was aware that he was learning.

This was not like learning in a classroom. When he had a realization he didn't wonder why. There was no logic to the understanding because everything was so perfectly clear. He knew why there was suffering, war, poverty and cruelty. He also understood clearly what his place was in the universe. He was connected to everything.

He smiled and realized it wasn't that he was connected to everything, he somehow was everything. Yet this also made perfect sense.

The angels of gold that he had seen earlier now returned. He felt the immediate love for them only this time he felt them loving him. A calmness and peace washed over his entire being. He knew that there was only one thing now and forever that really mattered and that was this love and peace. He knew he would try to stay here. He didn't want to go back to earth or his body. He knew instinctively and perfectly that his family would be fine. Their journey would continue.

The angels had stopped looking at him and turned towards each other. They were huddled around one another and appeared to be looking down. Bob moved to them. They were looking at his body and the doctors

working on him in the hospital. One of the angels looked directly at Bob and said

"Watch what I am doing."

Bob could once again see inside his hospital room. Now he was further away. The angel was directing something towards the doctor. It was an energy that guided right through the surgeon.

The angel then looked back to Bob again.

"This is one of the things that you need to remember. We can work through you in the same way. You must have faith, or someone has to want our help. This is how prayer works. Someone is praying for you right now. They are praying specifically for us to help you by helping the doctor."

He was then pulled away from the operating room and out of the hospital. He could see it rapidly disappearing below him. The angels had stayed behind and were still working. But they were too far for Bob to see clearly.

Now he was at the edge of enormous field of rolling green hills and flowers. The sky was a brilliant blue. He had a feeling of being in the biggest area he had ever seen. This field was somehow the entire universe and it was bigger than he could conceive even though he was looking at all of it. Everything just seemed enormous. And yet he felt a coziness.

He walked, or somehow moved through the field. If he saw it, he was there. If he thought about what he was looking at he was instantly next to it. Every blade of grass was perfect. It was perfectly formed and perfectly green. He could feel his feet as he walked on it but the grass was not damaged or changed in any way.

There was a large pond of to his left surrounded by a group of smaller trees and perfectly formed little bushes. At the edge of the pond there were three men fishing. Bob tilted his head to the side and listened to them talk. They were just talking about fishing. They were smiling and

having a wonderful time. The man in the middle noticed Bob and looked directly at him. Bob understood that this was a relative but he didn't know who it was. The man's smile faded. '

"You shouldn't be here yet Bobby."

And then he turned back to his fishing. The other men either didn't notice him, or didn't bother to address him. They just kept talking and fishing.

There were birds flying around the pond singing like no birds he had ever heard. As Bob kept staring he noticed a dog run up to the men. It was a beautiful brown and white collie. The man on the left bent down to pet the dog.

"Hey Duke, where have you been?" The other men smiled and stooped to pet the dog without dropping their fishing poles.

The dog sat and looked across the pond. The men's eyes followed. A young girl was riding a beautiful black horse. The joy in the girls' face made Bob smile. The muscles on the hoarse rippled under a sheen of sweat.

Bob was sure that the horse was smiling as well, but reasoned it may have just been enjoying the run. Would horses smile even in Heaven? All three of the men waved to the girl. She gave a small wave back, smiled and turned and ran off with the horse away from the pond.

On the other side of the field was a grove of trees. These were the fullest and most perfect trees Bob had ever seen. The leaves and the grass round them were all a vivid green. The trees were made of the some translucent material. It looked like wood yet somehow very different. It was if wood was a priceless gemstone. Through the trees a group of twenty or so people were singing and skipping. Bob thought that they might have been playing a game of some kind because they were laughing. Not chuckling, but laughing as if at the most hilarious joke they had ever heard.

There were boys and girls but they were dressed the same. They all wore a robe or gown made of a bright but very soft white linen. The youngest of the group was just a child of ten or eleven years old. The oldest might have been about thirty. But they were all beautiful.

A tree stood in the center of the field all by itself. The tree was very far away but in just an instant he was standing directly under it. Each leave was a different color. The colors were so vivid that he tried to stop at each single leave and take it in. The leaves appeared to be electric or neon. The colors were so bright that he was certain there must be a power source to them.

Some of the colors he had never seen before. He reached out to one leaf and let it rest in the palm of his hand. There was a droplet of water on the leaf. Inside the drop he could see even more colors. The drop was perfectly reflecting the millions of colors from every leaf on the tree. The single leaf felt like satin. It was so light that he could see his hand through the leaf.

Bob noticed a young girl standing beside the tree smiling at him. He walked towards her. She smiled and told him she would guide him. The girl was dressed in a green outfit that made him think of an elf. She appeared to be no more than eighteen or nineteen years old but her face reflected the wisdom of someone who had lived a very long and happy life. Her hair was black and her eyes were as green as the brightness of her clothes. The feeling of love was starting to overwhelm him.

He knew only one thing. He wanted to stay here and experience this love and this peace.

The girl spoke to him. But not with a normal voice. She was speaking inside his head.

"This is all built on love. You are feeling the love of everything."

Bob felt like a child again.

"I don't even think we define the word love correctly back on Earth. I want this love forever. I don't want to go back." He said.

"You are not finished. You have much more to do on Earth. Take as much of this love as you can back to Earth."

The girl was a stranger to Bob. He was sure he had never met her before. And yet he also knew that this was a soul mate. Someone he had known forever.

Then a group of people appeared behind her. He didn't know if they had been there all along and he hadn't noticed them or if they had appeared suddenly. As they came closer he began to recognize them.

Although his great grand-father had died when Bob was very young he recognized him instantly. He saw aunts and uncles and cousins he didn't even remember on Earth or who had died before he was even born. But he knew he was connected to them. They were all overjoyed at seeing him. They talked about things in his life. Events that at the time he felt had no significant meaning.

But now he understood that those events had a profound importance on his life. They were happy, painful and some even bland or boring events. Random interactions with strangers when he had done something nice or they had done something nice for him. He understood that this was a basis of love.

His father stepped forward. "You will have to go back Bobby. It is not time for you to be with us yet."

With that the group turned and walked away from him leaving him alone again.

BOB REVIEWS HIS LIFE

Now a man appeared walking towards them. He had shoulder length brown hair and a well-groomed beard. It was the man's eyes that grabbed Bob's focus. They were a brilliant blue green and the kindest eyes Bob had ever seen.

Everything that was around him had disappeared and he was in an area that was all white. There was substance to the room but the walls the floor and the ceiling were all of a brilliant clean white.

"Are you ready for your life review?" The man asked.

"Yes." Bob stammered. He somehow was aware of exactly what was going to happen.

A huge screen appeared in front of him. It looked like a flat screen television or movie screen but there was no depth or dimension to it. It simply floated in front of him.

In a single second he re-lived his entire life. The colors were vivid and he could absorb even the tiniest detail without a focused thought. He could see everything and feel everything. And even though he was watching it like a television he also felt like he was there. He was watching his life and experiencing it at the same time.

The very first scene was of him being born. A doctor was pulling Bob out of his mother. He could see his tiny hand holding on to the umbilical cord. He could watch it as an observer and yet still experience his birth as himself.

He was a tiny baby contemplating that his life was beginning. He knew that this was not his current mind and current self, experiencing his

own birth. It was his mind and consciousness as a tiny baby aware of exactly what was happening.

He saw himself in his mother's arms. He saw himself bouncing on his father's knee. As he grew older he experienced things he had done or said to people that were not very nice. The man standing next to him was experiencing Bob's life with him.

Bob felt as if he was inside the man's mind and the man was inside Bob's mind. But the man made no judgement of him. Bob was trying to judge himself but he could not.

He was however not hard on himself. He was simply acknowledging that the things he had done were not right and had not made the world a better place. He knew that he was supposed to learn from these events.

The other emotions mirrored what he had done in life. In one split second he was sitting in a classroom. He recognized his third grade teacher immediately. Her name was Mrs. Riggle and he would always remember her.

It was late in the school year and Bob had been struggling with his grades. His mom and dad had been fighting lately and were talking about divorce. Mrs. Riggle did not know this. She just knew that Bob wasn't doing well after having been a straight 'A' student. She had started to scold him and Bob began crying.

She had immediately taken him back to the cloak room. The little room at the back of the class that the kids put their coats in. She gently wiped his tears away and had a long talk with him. Her eyes never left his face. Bob could feel her emotions as if he were Mrs. Riggle. She felt hurt that she had upset this little boy.

When Bob told her his parents were fighting all the time and he though they were getting a divorce he felt her heart break. It was such a

strange feeling. Bob felt bad for himself in a way he could not say. He felt a compassion for himself as if he were a different person.

She told little Bobby how smart he was and what a good young man he was. She had made little jokes and talked to him like an adult about relationships and marriage. Then Bob re-lived walking back out of the room and into the classroom.

He could observe it, and yet feel it and be a part of it at the same time. He was that little child walking back in to the classroom and he was that child as a grown man watching the child. Yet this did not cause him any confusion.

He could understand perfectly how and why it was happening. All of the kids were now looking at him. Mrs. Riggle noticed Bobby's fear. She had her arm around him and made another little joke about paddling him. All of the kids started laughing and the drama was over. He would never forget her warmth and understanding.

He looked at the clock above the teacher's desk in the classroom and saw that in four minutes it would be three O'clock and the bell would ring. He felt the pure innocence of a child about to be released from class on a warm spring day. He re-lived that feeling that was so common to little kids. The utter joy of leaving school at the end of a long day and walking home with his friends.

And now he was in middle school. It was science class and the teacher was talking about sharks. The teacher, Sister Betty, was a kind nun in her late sixties who loved science, loved her students and loved teaching. When the topic of sharks came up she took advantage of the moment to let one particular student shine.

Paul Caparzo was the shark kid. He had big glasses, was tall and always had messy blond hair hanging in his eyes. Paul loved sharks. He talked about sharks every chance he got. Often other teachers would have

to take a book away from him about sharks because he was supposed to be studying history or English.

"Why don't we let our resident expert Paul tell us about some of the bigger more dangerous sharks?" Sister Betty said with a smile.

Paul's face lit up like he had won the Nobel Prize. The class starting laughing and one kid blurted out, "Oh no! We aren't going to listen to geek boy go on about stupid sharks are we?"

Paul's smile quickly faded and he began to shrink in to his own body. But just as quickly Bob yelled back. "Shut up man! Sharks are cool. And can you even spell shark?"

The smile went right back to Paul's face and he sat up in his seat and started to talk. Bob could hear the words but also feel the pride in Paul.

Then, as if in another corner of the screen Bob could see Paul today on a boat in the ocean. He remembered reading on Facebook that Paul was an oceanography professor. He knew he had played some small little part in it. But again he didn't feel anything other than a learning moment. He knew that when he encouraged people he somehow made the world a better place.

Just as quickly he was back on the steps of his high school. It was summer and school was getting ready to start. He knew where this was going and started to cringe before it even happened. His friend Jeff Barnes was walking away from the school with his mother. Bob noticed that over the summer Jeff had gotten an ear ring.

"Hey Jeff, did they give you a free skirt when you got that ear ring?" He yelled.

His other friends around him laughed at Bob's joke. Jeff turned around and just stared at him. "No, I don't think so." was all he said.

Bob remembered the scowl he had received from Jeff's mother. He and Jeff had never been best friends or particularly close. They worked together and occasionally nodded in the hallways between classes. But Bob always thought Jeff was one of the best kids in the class. He was genuinely nice, got better grades than Bob and seemed to have a really good life. For years the incident had stuck in Bob's mind. Why had he done it? Was it jealousy or was Bob just a jerk. As all of the thoughts were now racing through his mind he could also feel what Jeff was feeling and hear Jeff's thoughts.

Jeff hadn't been heart broken or embarrassed. He had simply felt let down. He was disappointed in Bob. He thought that he had wasted his time trying to be Bob's friend. And then Jeff had forgotten about the entire interaction. It meant nothing to him. But Bob also knew that it meant a lot to him. He had lost in one moment of stupidity a potential lifelong friend. He had lost a relationship that would have made his life better.

Then just as quickly he could see himself getting married and connecting to his wife Donna. He could feel Donna's love for him standing at the altar. The joy he felt brought a physical tear to his eye.

At the reception he re-lived the feeling of happiness. He recalled at the time that it was a strange feeling. So many of his relatives that he rarely saw were honestly and deeply happy for him. He understood that this was the essence of life.

These connections to other people were what matter more than anything. He also understood that his life, everyone's life, on Earth was just part of a bigger life and bigger connections. At the core of it all he knew was love. He allowed himself to just focus on watching the story of his life unfold.

He could not count how many times in his life he had interacted with other people. Some of them were family and friends. Others that were just as clear were small little interactions with complete strangers. He could feel what those people felt.

In one instant he was walking in a convenience store and an older lady was walking out. He had held the door for her and smiled at her and said what a beautiful day it was. It was one little sentence. But it had made the lady happy.

Bob now knew that her husband had died just a few weeks ago and her children all lived far away from her and had gone back home after the funeral. He could see the lady's eyes brighten and the big smile on her face. A simple mention of what a beautiful day it was had brought joy and hope to her.

In the same instant, at the same time he was leaving a familiar restaurant after eating lunch. Walking out of the door next to him was a young man of about twenty-two years old. Bob recognized the man as someone who had cut him off as he was pulling in to the parking lot. As they were now leaving Bob gave the young man an evil look. He said to himself in his mind,

"Yeah you jerk. You just had to get five seconds in front of me so you could eat first and yet here we are leaving at the exact same moment."

Now Bob could also feel exactly what the man was feeling. The man had lowered his head when he saw Bob's glance. It was if Bob was now him. He could think his thoughts.

The man had just lost his job. His wife was worried and they had a baby daughter that he needed to take care of. The man had gone to the restaurant to meet a friend about a potential job and he was running late so he had cut Bob off to get there as quickly as possible. But the friend had texted him that he wouldn't be able to make it. It caused Bob's heart to sink.

The next thought the man had made it even worse. He wasn't despondent about not seeing his friend and the loss of the job opportunity. The man felt bad for cutting Bob off.

And still Bob did not judge himself. Although he could feel the sadness he had caused and the pain he had caused it was somehow disconnected. He knew that some of things that he had thought about for years, things that he was certain had made other people feel bad weren't that important.

There were other times when he had thought nothing of an interaction yet it had had a profound influence on people either good or bad. He just observed these incidents and filed them away as something he should learn from.

A sudden terror gripped him, but just as quickly passed. He was standing outside of The Children's hospital in Cincinnati Ohio. His daughter had just been diagnosed with a rare heart defect. He could see himself doubled over and sobbing.

Cassidy was only six months old. She didn't even have a chance to start her life and now she could be dead tomorrow. The surgery was already scheduled. Her aorta had developed wrapping itself around her trachea and was slowly suffocating her. There was no time for a second opinion and this hospital had the best pediatric heart team in the nation. The surgery would be dangerous but they had a high level of success. If it worked, she could go on to live a normal life. If it didn't she would die.

There were two things Bob felt simultaneously. He knew the surgery had been a success and Cassidy was the happiest little girl in the world. He also knew that if she had died, she would have been in Heaven. Both thoughts brought a smile to his face.

He reviewed the rest of his life in the same instant. Everything seemed to happen at the speed of light, and yet he could understand all of it. He went through losing his job and the financial troubles. He went through getting his current job. He re-lived that moment in the garage when he fell to his knees and started praying. He was then at the new company meeting people he would work with and understanding his interactions with every single one of them.

He could instantly recall and analyze every single waiter or convenience store cashier or stranger on a sidewalk and understand the interaction.

Just as quickly as it began he saw himself walking out to his Corvette. He knew this was today. And the review of his life was over.

The man who was guiding him now looked deep into Bob's eyes and spoke in that spiritual voice. "Now you will meet Samuel but I will see you again when it is your time. Hold on to what you have seen here and live your life to have fun, be happy, connect with other people and love."

He was out of the white room and back in the fields where his journey had begun.

He was aware of his father again standing near him. His dad again had a stern look on his face.

"You cannot stay here Bobby, you have to go back. It isn't time for you to come home yet."

Then the other members of his family appeared and looked down to the ground. They pointed and nodded.

"He's right Bobby it isn't your time." One of them said.

BOB SEES A CITY IN HEAVEN

H e made a slight step forward but was stopped. Not by a person or angel but by some barrier he could not quite see. He knew he wasn't really in Heaven. He was in the welcome room, or a holding area. He knew that something was beyond the barrier and that he could not cross it. For if he did he was sure he could never return to his life on Earth.

The tree caught his eye again off to his left. Why did these people keep telling him he had to go back? He wanted to see the tree again and the thought alone was enough to propel him back to it. Beyond the tree was a hill and on the hill was a city. He could see people moving around in the city between buildings.

The buildings were of an architecture he had never seen before. They were made of a gold brick and appeared to glow. Around the city was a stream with the most beautiful flowers he had ever seen lining the banks. A bridge made of what looked like crystal and pearl crossed the stream into the city.

He walked to the middle of the bridge and looked at the stream. The water was blue and transparent as the cleanest glass. Brightly colored fish swam lazily. The flowers along the banks were offset with a brilliant green grass. He had never seen flowers quite so vivid before.

Beyond the bridge and into the city he could see spirits walking along paths next to the golden buildings. He could see what he thought must be churches. These were the color of beautiful gems. Some were ruby

red while others were emerald green or sapphire blue. The churches gave off a light that came from within them.

Some of the buildings had domes of brilliant colors. Other buildings were huge skyscrapers. But around the buildings were what looked to be little fairy tale villages. And from everything came the light. The light was just as much a part of the city as the buildings.

He did not speak or ask any questions. But he knew that the people, the spirits he could see in the city, were working. Some were welcoming people who had recently died. Others were working with humans on earth.

He could see beings going back and forth between Earth and the city. He could also see people in the city interacting with the Earth. A man was dropping a thin silver dime to show one of his loved ones back on Earth that he was still with him. Another was putting a freshly picked flower in the path of his still living wife as she walked along a familiar trail.

The city appeared to be endless and yet he could still get a physical sense of the buildings and the people who were living in it. They were all perfectly happy. It was the only way to describe it. The beings, the people in the city were filled with so much joy that the city itself was joy.

He had a strange feeling that he had always known this city. It was the perfect city and he thought that every building, every flower and every fish swimming in the stream was completely perfect. If there were a perfect city on earth this is what it would look like.

The city seemed to him to be infinite in size yet he could also sense the barrier. The line that he could not cross. He stepped back just off the bridge away from the city and just stood silently to admire the beauty. This is what nature looked like when it was perfect. The buildings all fit perfectly in with nature.

The city represents the world. He understands this completely and yet he cannot articulate how or why. The people are as different as they are in a major metropolitan city like New York, London or Paris. And yet they are the same. They are human beings. The angels are different from one another, and yet they are the same. They are connected deeply and entirely.

He knew that the two were connected. The city here and the world and its cities and buildings. He didn't know if this was by design of the city, or if people on Earth somehow had a connection to this city and built buildings to try to be the same. The churches and cathedrals looked like beautiful paintings of ancient European churches. But they were even more beautiful. They were more colorful and certainly brighter. Everything was brighter.

At the front of the city he could see a massive door. The door was easily fifty feet high and several feet thick. A man stood outside the door and would smile and open it for people who were coming in from where Bob was. He wondered what it took to get through that door. He knew he would walk through some day, but that he couldn't yet.

Then Bob became aware of the music. He had occasionally listened to classical music. Nothing he had ever heard could compare to this. He recognized some of the instruments. There were clearly horns like trumpets or trombones. He could distinctly hear violins, harps and other stringed instruments. Many of the sounds were new to him. And all of the notes were new. Just like the city the music was perfect. He could not only hear the music he could somehow feel the vibrations in his body. Even though the sound was soft he could hear it clearly.

His father and family were now beside him. They started to back away from him. It was just a few steps. Enough to indicate that he couldn't follow them. And then another bright light descended.

The light filled everything around him. He felt it and his smile grew wider.

And then another man was standing before him. Bob titled his head to the side contemplating this new visitor. He was of average height, had silvery gray hair but neatly groomed and a well-groomed beard. His eyes were a blue gray. This, Bob knew, was an angel.

Bob heard a voice and stood perfectly still. The voice did not come from the angel who had appeared but from somewhere else.

"Many who come this far are given a choice. You will have to go back." The man said. "But first you will continue this journey,"

The authority in the voice was perfect. Bob knew this had to be the voice of God. No one else could speak with such complete authority. It was the only word he could think of. This voice could move mountains. This voice could create the universe. This voice was never wrong and knew everything.

BOB MEETS AN ANGEL

or the first time since his death Bob felt himself starting to frown.

"But why do I have to go back?" He asked innocently.

The angel answered. "The people have lost their way. They are living one life, the physical life. It is time for them to reconnect to the other half, the spiritual life. You will help them to make that connection. You have many questions and many on earth have the same questions. I will answer these questions and then you will go back and tell people the truth.

You will not be alone in this mission. Others, every day, are having similar experiences. They will help. You will understand and remember almost everything that I tell you and when I am finished your mind and soul and body will be put back together."

Bob felt naked and afraid. Seconds before he knew exactly who he was. There was no pretense at all in any thought or word. Now he was as he had been before he died. He brought his hands to his face and lowered his head.

He rubbed his temples. He was a physical human being again. He felt no pain but his human emotions returned. He had his ego back. He had that edge of pretense shared by all humans. He was still very comfortable but the pure joy and childish exuberance were gone. The understanding of everything was gone.

He was moving again. The angel and Bob were now sitting on large rocks high up in some foreign land. The land around them was brown but down below and off in the distance he could see beautiful mountain ranges and green valleys. He appreciated the beauty, but at the same time knew that it wasn't complete. His return to his human self was hiding something. The view calmed his mind and he had his first realization.

"This is what is meant by Adam and Eve discovering they were naked isn't it?" He asked.

"Yes. When man made the decision to be separated from God and the spiritual world their eyes were suddenly open. They knew that without God they were alone. This is what free will feels like without guidance and purpose. This is why two people can be in the middle of thousands and one can feel terribly alone and the other, who may not know a single person around him can smile and know that he is not alone."

"But the truth is that we are never alone are we?" Bob asked.

He surprised himself with the sudden revelation. He knew things. He felt things and he saw things differently than he had just minutes earlier. But he couldn't pull it all together. Some critical piece of the puzzle was missing. There was a key to a door that he could not find.

"No. God will always be with you if you seek him." The man answered. "The entire fall is from the simple addition of free will. You now can be free from God. We do not want this but you have asked for it and it has been granted."

Bob sat quietly for a moment and so did the man. He wanted to ask the man who he was but was afraid of the answer. Before he could think of the next question the man spoke again.

"You will have many questions and we will have time to discuss them.

Bob lowered his head. He wished he hadn't had his body, mind, and soul put back together, or whatever it was that the man had done to him.

He liked it better when he was stripped of his pretense and ego. With those things back he now had anxiety. The first question should have been the easiest. He decided to just ask.

"Are you God?"

The man laughed heartily tossing his head back and covering his mouth with his hand.

"No I am not. I'm sorry Bob I should have told you from the start. My name is Samuel. I am what you would call an Angel. What that really means is that I have not lived on earth in a physical form. I and many others were created by God long before you were. We work now to guide humans on Earth.

The girl you met would be the type of being who would guide you in Heaven. But since you are not beyond the barrier I will guide you and teach you. You have more important questions and you are afraid to ask. These questions will be answered. Nothing is off limits and no question is unimportant. Before we begin in earnest I want you to continue the process that others will take when they die.

I want you to see and feel the entire experience of entering the spiritual world. You are at the barrier. You felt this when you saw the city, do you remember?"

Bob nodded and Samuel continued.

"That barrier can never be crossed by someone who is going back to earth. For many who come this far they do not get a choice. They are not ready to cross the barrier. Others get a choice. They may cross the barrier and stay or they can go back. The city connects Earth to Heaven. So you can see it and walk through it. You can experience everything on this side of the barrier.

The reason for this is rather simple. It prepares you not for entry to Heaven but to return to Earth. This is where Earth and Heaven connect.

To live on Earth you must have free will. The barrier stops you from seeing all of Heaven and truly experiencing life as it really is. If you crossed the barrier you would lose your free will. You would be frozen in your thoughts just waiting to get to Heaven."

"I don't think I understand." Bob said.

"There are certain things you need to learn on Earth. You must learn to love other people. You must have an open heart. Heaven is for eternity. Remember how great you felt just standing outside that city? Remember how wonderful you felt and how much love you felt when you first saw angels and loved ones from your life?

Heaven is many times greater. If you cannot get along and love your fellow humans because they have a different skin color or speak a different language how are you going to fare in Heaven? You have heard it before, 'Love your enemies' why do you think that is?" Samuel asked.

"I guess because we are supposed to love everyone and that includes our enemies." Bob replied.

Samuel continued. "You should love everyone. But the particular point of loving your enemies is that if you do, you will quickly find out that you don't have as many enemies as you thought you did.

When you had the accident that brought you here you were trying to make a phone call to Jim Stahlhaber. That is a man you consider your enemy. The first thing you did when you had the accident was curse him under your breath. You consider him an enemy. And while he may not be a very happy person, and he may do things to you that he shouldn't, have you ever tried to just love him as a human being? Have you ever tried to connect with him to understand him better?"

Bob bowed his head and tried to think. The first thought that came to him was, "this is going to be harder than I thought." He did not like Jim Stahlhaber at all and couldn't imagine trying to love him.

"I'm sorry Samuel, but I hate that guy."

Bob immediately cringed. He had just told an angel of God that he hated another human being. For a brief second his body tensed as he waited to be cast back into Earth or even worse. The reaction from Samuel was not what he expected. Samuel burst out in laughter. Bob's anxiety quickly turned to confusion as Samuel continued to laugh. After a moment Bob began to smile at the pure joy of Samuel's happiness.

"How can you hate a man you do not know?"

Samuel shook his head back and forth with a broad smile still set on his face.

"This is what so many people do. You fill yourself with what you think is hatred when it is actually just ignorance. You cannot possibly hate what you do not know. It is completely illogical Bob.

If you hate him you don't have to bother with working to understand or know him. It's the lazy way to misery. Of course the problem for you is that hate hurts you and it doesn't help Jim Stahlhaber or anyone else who you hate. It just consumes you with anger.

One of the worst things you can do to a person is to get them to hate you. It gives them so much power over your life. When a person hates you he fears you. When a person fears you he will do anything to make the fear go away. When you fill yourself with hate it doesn't leave much room for love. When you have no love it becomes impossible to be happy. You are consumed by fear and hate. It sits at the back of your mind. You may forget about it for a while. But it will always return.

When you had your life review what did you see?"

Bob thought for a second. "It was mostly good times and good things I had done in my life. But there were also times where I saw myself making a bad decision or hurting someone. In those moments I could feel what I had done to that person. It wasn't a judgement. I just felt like I should have

learned something from it that made my life happier and the other person happier."

"How many times in that review did you see Jim Stahlhaber?"

"Well, I didn't see him at all."

"What does that tell you Bob?"

Bob began laughing as hard as Samuel had when he first told him he hated Jim. He understood it completely. "I think that me hating Jim is the dumbest thing I have ever done. It didn't affect him at all and it was a complete waste of my time."

His laughter began to grow. "I mean, what was I thinking? I wasted my time hating someone who I have probably spent four hours with my entire life. I don't really know him at all. It made me angry, it didn't help him and I spent probably twice as much time hating him as I ever did even talking to him. Why did I ever do something so obviously stupid?"

"Ahhhh! An excellent question Bob. And one that far too many humans don't bother to ask.

The answer is simple. You don't spend enough time thinking about your life. You spend a lot of your time thinking about the things you have or want. You don't spend any time at all thinking about your life itself. When you think about the future you focus too much on what you will have or not have. You think about the physical and the material, or what other people will think about you.

But it gets worse Bob. Because when you are motivated by what other people will think you don't spend enough energy on building your own character. You don't build your foundation. Character is doing what you say you will do and doing the things you know need to be done. Integrity is doing these things well. When a bad thing happens you only fix it enough so other people won't notice. You are spending your life worried the show you put on for others won't be believed. That's what it really

comes down to. You are worried they will actually know the truth about you. So you spend energy creating a life that isn't real. A life that you want other people to think is your life. The result is misery."

"It's weird Samuel." Bob said.

"What's weird?"

"We were just laughing about how I hated Jim, and how stupid that was. I guess I never thought there would be humor in Heaven. I like that I can laugh honestly and easily"

Samuel smiled briefly and continued talking.

"What if you put as much effort on thinking about how happy you can be in the future? What if you put effort into being a better person?

What if you put effort and focus into thinking about how you could make other people happy?

If those around you were happier wouldn't it logically follow that you would be happier? If you did that and other people saw you and your life, and knew it was the truth, wouldn't you be happier?

If you spent your energy on building your own character and integrity you will be both a better person and a happier person. You will be able to weather storms when they come and find your joy more quickly.

Doing things well. Living life with your head up and confronting challenges is what every person wants to do. It gives you an inner peace. It gives you value of self. Too many people do things well not for the experience. They do things well to get stuff.

You're changing the goal to something that is not very important. When you make this change you lose the value gained from the experience.

If you focus and work hard to solve a problem and you are successful it can be very rewarding not just right now, but for the rest of your life. The things that you learned cannot be taken away from you. If you do the exact same thing but your goal is not to fix the problem, but to be rewarded with some material possession for fixing the problem you won't work as hard, you won't learn as much and your foundation will be weak. You will only work hard enough to get the material reward.

When you do that you have no connection to the action, just the result. So you don't learn as much. You don't build character or integrity and you don't increase your value. Eventually you will pay a price for all of those shortcuts. You will pay that price on Earth and you will pay that price when you are done with this Earth.

Heaven is forever. You cannot be in Heaven and lack character or integrity. Would you want a mean person in Heaven? Would you want a lazy person in Heaven?

Maybe the simpler question is; do you want them around you on Earth? If the answer is no it should tell you something. If you don't want them around temporarily you certainly won't want them around forever. There is a more difficult connection. Do you think people would want to be around you forever?

Love is what makes all of this work. Not things. Love connects the work to people. Love connects actions to rewards. You want to know what love really is. It is connections.

Bob shook his head again stunned by such a simple revelation. "How could I have possibly failed to understand this? It is so simple and obvious."

Samuel answered quickly.

"How often have you thought about it? What I am going to do is give you information that you will take back with you that will answer

some of these questions. Then when you think about your life and your future you won't be distracted wondering about why you are here in the first place or what you perceive to be the bigger connection in life.

There are only three things that you need to understand and those three things will free your mind to focus on the importance of life. The things that bring happiness, joy and love to your life. The things you can focus on to make life fun. Not just for you but for everyone you interact with.

The three simple things are the foundation of understanding. When you have the settled in your mind you can focus on your purpose in life. That purpose of course is just to connect and love other people, and to enjoy this life. The end result is you make Earth more like Heaven. That's all there is to it. When you have a foundation the why becomes easier to understand. You are on Earth to build yourself. What you build allows you to get into Heaven. "

THE THREE THINGS

You are now at the threshold. This is the point where you would either return to Earth or begin your afterlife. Millions have seen what you have just seen. They have felt what you have felt. Many of these people were chosen as you were and they have returned to Earth to spread this message of life and love. You will be one of the few who will learn a little more. We will answer questions that you would have had in your Earthly body.

"There are three things that you must understand clearly to gain wisdom. All three of these things have been in front of you for your entire life but you have ignored them or not thought about what these three things really mean to you and all people. All three of these things will work together to strengthen you and help you to understand."

The First Thing

"The first thing you must know is that in the beginning there was nothing. This was written thousands of years ago and yet it has only been in the last few decades that you have begun to understand how profound it is.

There was nothing and now there was everything. Everything was created, and you, a thinking, rational intelligent human being can also create.

This is what the atheists and agnostics who believe they value science over God struggle with. They know 'what' was created. They may feel that God created science but they cannot understand how. So they will turn away from God and split themselves.

Many are simply turning away because they cannot understand how they got here. They believe that if they cannot understand how they got here, then there must be no purpose to their lives. This creates a vast emptiness that is hard to fill.

They will live only in the physical and destroy their spiritual. That of course leads to the question why? If you could figure out what was created, and figure out how it was created you would still be left with the most important question. Why?

'Why', is the hardest part isn't it? We can see the 'what'. You can use microscopes and telescopes to see and measure what was created. You can use technology to start to understand even some of the 'how'. But the 'why' is not so easy.

The problem with the 'why' question is that it leads back to more 'what' questions. And if you cannot know why you were created, how can you know what to do now that you are here?

If you live your life without having a goal or a purpose you cannot possibly have a plan for living your life."

Bob raised his hand to stop Samuel. "I think I'm getting confused. I watch and read things about the universe occasionally. But I'm no expert on it and I don't really think about it too much. I guess I just figured God made it for his own reasons but it really doesn't affect my life so I don't worry about it."

Samuel answered him quickly.

"In the beginning there was nothing but that doesn't mean there was no God and it doesn't mean that God had not created. It just means that the physical dimension that you live in now did not exist. At the split second of creation everything in the Universe was there.

And it wasn't just the material that was needed to create everything in the universe, it was the information. The blue print was

already there. The information for nuclear fusion to create all of the elements and the information needed to create a body and mind for your soul to exist within was in that tiny speck.

When you begin to understand this you will begin to slowly understand that time itself did not exist. When you die and leave your body, as you have now Bob, time does not exist. When you leave your earthly body you are. You exist within everything and you are connected to everything. In the beginning there was no physical dimension. Now there are new physical dimensions and they are connected to the spiritual dimensions. In the beginning there is nothing,

Why is this important Bob?"

Bob just shrugged his shoulders. He knew of the Big Bang Theory, He knew that The Bible said in the beginning there was nothing. But he had no idea why this was so important.

"If you were in that tiny space. If you were a part of that instant of creation doesn't it show you something?

You are that creation. You are as important to this universe as every grain of sand on the beach, of every star and every galaxy. All of it was connected.

You are as important as every king that ever lived. You are connected. You are connected to the leaders of the world, the billionaire businessmen, the movie star and the poor beggar you see on the side of the highway.

Every single one of you was created in the same way and with the same blue print for life. And at one point the matter that makes you up was indistinguishable from the matter that makes up every other human being. You were closer to them than you were to your own mother while you were in her womb."

Bob's mouth was open and his eyes were wide. This made sense. He knew the words Samuel had spoken were true. He knew it with his mind. This wasn't even spiritual. He had read these things in science books. He had heard of the singularity. When all of the universe was compressed into an infinitely small space.

He stood up and Samuel stood with him. They were in darkness. The only things that he could see were Samuel and Earth off in the distance. The image was of the familiar blue ball he has seen in photos taken from the moon. And yet it was so much clearer. He could feel the earth and everything that lived on the earth. He could feel an overwhelming connection.

This planet, this universe, and every living thing were connected. He knew it. He could see it and he could feel it. He also knew logically and clearly that if there was no universe in the beginning then everything was still connected to Heaven. This occurrence was not a religious thought. It was not spiritual. It was simply logical.

As quickly as he had stood and seen the earth from space he and Samuel were back on the planet. They were sitting in comfortable chairs on the top of a mountain range. All around him were sharp, snowcapped peaks. The wind blew but he was not cold.

Far below he could make out a small city. It was more of a village with perhaps a few dozen buildings. A clear pond was at the center and he could see flowing streams and roads. They were too high up to see people but he knew they were there.

A large black bird flew just a few feet away from them. Bob watched as the bird made wide circles around them. Its eyes seemed to be focused directly on him. He watched it for a few moments disinterested. Just enjoying its flight and the scenery surrounding him. He grew impatient. He thought that surely Samuel was trying to show him something. To teach him something through this beautiful bird and the incredible scene around him.

"Why did you bring me here Samuel?"

"I just think it's pretty." Was Samuel's simple answer. "We angels enjoy beauty and creation as much as you do."

The Second Thing

Both sat silently and watched the bird and stared at the mountains. Bob was still struggling with the craziness of time. Or more precisely the lack of time. Had they just been staring for a few brief seconds? Or had they been watching for hours? He could not describe the duration of any event.

Samuel continued talking.

"The second thing is that you were created in God's image. This does not mean that you look like God it means that you were created to think and to appreciate and value the things that God values. Things that are important to you are important to God. Things that you find beautiful God finds beautiful. But perhaps the most important is that you were created to love as God loves.

Most people today get the word love wrong. They think in terms of romantic love, or love for their children. Love is much more encompassing when it is from God and through God. There is no heartbreak in the love of God. Through meditation, prayer you can begin to understand what the image of God means to you.

When do you think that God was most pleased with you Bob?"

Bob looked up to the sky to collect his thoughts and then busted out laughing. The man started laughing too.

"You were looking to heaven for answers and to collect your thoughts and then you realized you were already here didn't you?"

Bob shook his head and smiled. Then he tried to answer the question.

"I know I'm no great person but I do try to help people from time to time. I've given bums on the street money and donated to charities."

"These are wonderful things and God appreciates them. But that is not the correct answer. When you were a young man you took your car on a long trip to visit a friend. At the time you were having difficulties with your father. You had been arguing with him and your mother about what job you should do and whether or not you should go to college. Do you remember this?"

Bob nodded that he remembered but had no idea where this was going.

"You left very early in the morning before the sun was up. About an hour into your trip you made a phone call to your dad. Do you remember now?"

And then Bob remembered but he was very confused.

"Yes, I remember. I called him because I was driving through an area with no houses or other cars on the road. I looked to the east and the sun was coming up between two hills. In front of the hills there was a big pond with a light fog over it. In the break of little patches through the fog I could see the sunlight glinting off of the water. It was spring and I remember seeing flowers along the pond and the green grass and trees on the hills. I remember the red and purple from the sunrise and how absolutely beautiful it was. I remember I wanted to call my dad and try to patch things up a little bit but I also wanted him to know how beautiful it was.

Is that what made God happy that I tried to patch things up with my dad?"

"That was pleasing to God as well as your charity. But what made God smile was the appreciation of the beauty. That is one important part of you being made in God's image. This is something that is also very obvious to all people and yet few acknowledge it.

If you knew nothing at all about God you would know that he likes to create things. If you look up through a telescope you see that God creates. There is so much of creation to see that it appears through the telescope to be endless. If you look down through the microscope the picture is the same. A single drop of water from a stream contains creation.

God likes to create things. The creations of the very small are as numerous as the unimaginably large. But when you appreciate the beauty and love that you see it opens your heart and your mind. The beauty is what allowed you to connect with your father.

All creative work is beautiful and all meaningless work is destructive. If you want to be happy and you want God to be with you, work creatively and recognize the beauty of God's work and the work of other people. You should love the beauty of creative work as you love your brother or your parents."

"If that work is done well it helps those I love. So I should also work on my children and my family." Bob interjected.

Yes. Your family and your children are also creations. And they are something that you constantly work on.

But that work is different. It is the work of love over a long period of time. They bring more joy to you over the entire course of your life. They complete and become the purpose of the other work that you do. In fact, as you saw your family is what made that moment complete. If you had done the same amount of work and created something that was good, but you didn't have people you loved to benefit from the work it would have been meaningless.

There are many people on Earth who work very hard and have great integrity in their work. They create beautiful things. These things may make other people happy.

But for them that is not what drives the creation. They are creating and working to make more and more money. To buy more things and for them, most importantly, they have these things to show other people their greatness. Not the greatness of the thing they have created. And so these people are often not very happy. They have created but they have created for the wrong reasons. The sadness and sometimes misery that they feel is because they know they have accomplished something that required hard work. But they did it for the wrong reasons. They have no end purpose to the creation. To be happy and to create a better world, everything that you create must have a purpose beyond yourself and money.

The Third Thing

"The third important thing for you to understand is, "I AM." This is what Moses was told when he asked God who he was.

Notice how concise and perfect the sentence is. There is nothing left to add to it and everything in the universe can be added to it. When you concentrate on just that thought, that when God says 'I am.' It means everything. Any word you put after 'I am' works. 'I am' also tells you exactly your place in the universe.

When you first arrived here you knew clearly that you were connected to every single thing that exists in the universe. And even though I have hidden things from you right now so that you can understand these things in a physical sense you still know it don't you?"

"Yes." Bob said. That is the part of this that I think will stick with me the most. I know somehow that I am connected to everyone else and everything."

"If you understand that simple fact you will also understand that you must be connected to God."

These three things will frame everything else we talk about Bob. You should think of them as you think of God. This universe was created by God. God values creation and appreciation of creation which you call beauty. God created everything, you were created in God's likeness and God is everything.

Now to tie all three things together there is any obvious question. Why did God do this? The answer is love. All of creation is an act of love. Everything that is connected is connected with love. When you first passed into this side you felt that overwhelming love. It gets bigger and you will feel even more love. Love is the music that ties together the three symphonies.

When you understand those three simple things you will not wish to live your life separated from God. But you will also understand that your life does have a purpose. You are not here by accident. You are here to fulfill the connection. You are here some days to be the person who by some seemingly meaningless act connects other people with love.

Some days your purpose is to be affected by another person. You fulfill your connection and strengthen the love you feel and the love you express. These things are necessary to complete the experience. When you pull away from love you lose the connection and bad things begin to happen. God doesn't pull away from you, but he will go away if you ask."

"I've always pulled away from God. I know that now." Bob said.

"But I've also tried to keep my faith. When I do something that I think may have a right or wrong I always try to do the right thing. I don't always succeed but I know when I have done something wrong. I also make excuses for myself. I understand the three things you have told me. I really understood them the second I got here.

Now I know they are important and I know why. What I don't understand is why so much science is dedicated to proving God doesn't exist. I mean, I'm not a scientist or anything. But a lot of really smart people don't believe in God. And now that I know it is all real I can't help but wonder why it is like this?

Was it always this way? Did people always feel a little embarrassed to talk about their faith or to talk about God?"

"No," Samuel responded, "in many ways it was even worse. People had a specific perception of God or a specific religion. They weren't afraid of talking about God, they were afraid of talking about God in the wrong way.

In very ancient times people would separate God. They believed that one God, or one part of God was in charge of the oceans, another in charge of the wind and on and so on. But they knew that the gods were connected. When they saw bad things happen with the weather they assumed the weather god was mad at them, or that the gods were fighting among themselves.

They didn't understand how things worked. Yet even through those times God was with them and they knew this. They could feel it.

At the same time there were just as many people who believed there was only one god. Different groups believed different things and that would cause conflict. If you study the past you will find that they were using religion as a reason to increase their own wealth or power.

Those who believe God is love and that they are here to help and learn don't wish to fight or gain power over one another. They understand that this will not make them happy and does not fulfill their purpose.

The three things I have told you have always been known. They are just not kept as part of your life. Religion often tries to take those three things and make them much more complicated than they actually are.

Many today are running not from God but from their perception or belief of what they are supposed to be doing on Earth. They believe that if God is real that they must always be submissive and suffering so that they can get into Heaven.

Why would God create man just to suffer? And when you feel love, how can one possibly believe that love and misery can be created by the same God?

There has always been the pain of loss and separation. And other than physical pain the pain of loss and separation is the only pain that exists. If you separate your life in to just the physical world and you reject the spiritual world, God and love then of course you will be in misery. Death for them is a permanent separation and a permanent loss. Do you believe that death is permanent Bob?"

Bob had to laugh out loud. "Of course not! I am here and I know that this is real!"

"Of course it is. And for thousands of years almost everyone knew that it was real. They knew that this life is temporary. They knew that there was something else. So the pain of loss and the pain of separation were always temporary.

When you live a life away from the truth it's hard to be happy. What's even worse is that one must work very hard to turn away from that truth.

God isn't hiding Bob. He is everywhere. Every single day God interacts with all of us and often in very profound ways. The experience you are having right now has been experienced by millions and millions of people. They were close to dying. They were brought to this point and shown these things. They remember much of it and they go back to Earth and tell the story.

There are millions of other stories where an angel shows up! And yet you say God is hiding. It isn't God who is hiding. It is people who are hiding."

WHY IS THERE SO MUCH SUFFERING?

Before Bob asked his next question he thought about his daughter and how much he wanted her to be happy. He also thought about how sick she had been as a baby. For a few weeks they thought she would not survive. The pain he felt had almost pushed him over the edge. He was trying to ask the question intelligently. He wanted his words to be clear so that the answer would be clear. There was only one way to ask such a question. He had to just ask.

"Why is there so much suffering on earth? "

Samuel answered quickly.

"Every life is extremely important. But life on Earth is only part of life. I'm going to show you something now.

Look behind you."

Bob turned and saw that he was in New York City. There were people everywhere but they did not notice him. He saw many people that were stressed out about something. It was clear in their faces and their posture. Others were talking on the phone smiling and joyous. Still others appeared to be walking in a world by themselves.

"Turn around again."

Bob turned again and saw a pond with men standing around fishing. One of the men was his father. None of them noticed Bob.

"They are here to enjoy this earth as it was always meant to be enjoyed." Samuel said. "For them there is no suffering, only love and joy.

Even in the big city on Earth you saw people that were enjoying life. They were in their physical bodies. They have suffering and pain their lives. But they only let it get to a certain point. They know that it cannot invade the spiritual side of life. They learn from it and it allows them to be happier.

The Earth is not heaven. You can be "dead" as you would call it and still be on earth. But when you are in your physical body and you are on earth you are in a good place, but you are not in a perfect place. Some things that happen on Earth happen because it is not perfect. The reason that it is not perfect is because you made the Earth what it is. God made the physical Earth and he created human beings. You have free will to create the type of Earth that you want to live in. "

"This still doesn't explain why there is suffering and pain." Bob protested.

"I am going to separate you from your earthly body again." Samuel said.

The feeling of joy washed over Bob as it had when he first died. He had no ego, no sense of self and no desire but to enjoy this feeling. He said the first thing that came to his mind.

"I don't want to go back! I want to stay here. Don't tell me anything else just let me stay here!"

The angel Samuel smiled softly. "You cannot. I had to let you feel this again."

As quick as it had come it was gone and Bob knew he was back to himself. Or rather who he thought he was on Earth.

"Do you understand now?" Samuel asked.

"Yes. There is no amount of suffering I wouldn't endure to feel like this. The suffering is just temporary."

"True, but there is more to it than that." Samuel said.

"The suffering is necessary so that you may have free will. But much of it is a result of free will and the decisions people have made for themselves and people have made that affects others. If life on earth were perfect you would know that God is in control and you would live in constant supplication.

You cannot have free will if the master is always over you. God does not want that and you do not want that. You cannot go and create if you cannot make decisions. It also goes with your spiritual self. Your physical body can be perfectly healthy and free of pain but your spiritual self can be in anguish. The opposite is also just as true. You see this in your life. People who are riddled with cancer or some other ailment yet they are still happy. Their spiritual self is healthy.

There is something else that you must consider. When someone is in pain or dies there is always sadness. It is never easy.

The question is; would you want it to be easy? Of course not. It is hard because someone has died or is suffering that you love. You feel that connection with those that you love most at a time of suffering. Do not take that to mean suffering is good. It is not. You must put it in the place it belongs. It is temporary, there is often a reason behind it and it often leads to better things.

When you first arrived I told you that people were living one life and that they had to reconnect. A person cannot be happy with just a physical life. He is incomplete. You must live your life physically and spiritually. Then you will know peace. The way to do that is through love.

If you only live your physical life the suffering consumes you. If you connect the spiritual half of your life to your physical self the suffering can only go so far.

The spiritual life is the connection to the rest of God's creation. Many doors have been open yet many people will not walk through them. Many brilliant scientists understand that everything is connected. Yet they themselves will not make the connection."

Bob thought for a moment.

"I understand that all of us will suffer and feel pain at some point in our lives. But what about the people that never seem to have a good day. Sometimes when I'm walking in the city I'll see a homeless person. It looks like they've never had a good meal. Other times I'll see young kid in a wheelchair completely paralyzed. Or even someone who is mentally retarded. When I see these people I say; 'there but for the grace of God go I'. What about them? Why did they not get the grace of God?

Samuel laughed heartily. "How are you so sure they aren't happy? Let's be honest Bob, this isn't the only time you have said those words. In fact the last time you said that you said it under your breath. Do you remember?"

Bob looked puzzled. "No. I don't"

Samuel showed him another seen from his life and Bob remembered it instantly. It had happened just a few weeks before the accident. He was driving in his wife's mini-van with the entire family. They had gone grocery shopping and the check engine light had come on indicating another problem.

He had started to feel depressed about his financial problems when he passed a family in an old beat up station wagon. The car was not only dented and rusty but was also loud and throwing out smoke from the exhaust pipe. He looked over and saw the husband smiling and nodding

and a wife next to him chatting on about something. In the back seat he had noticed four or five kids from a small toddler to the oldest who looked to be a boy of sixteen or seventeen.

Bob remembered clearly now. He had said, "There but for the grace of God go I" under his breath. Money was tight but at least he didn't have five kids to feed and a beat up old junker to have to drive them around. He felt embarrassed for the man. He thought of pulling into his upper middle-class neighborhood in that old station wagon.

He recalled every bit of the event but still couldn't grasp Samuel's point.

"Ok yes. I remember now. And I guess I'm still glad for the grace of God. I mean, I understand that these people weren't paralyzed or living a life of poverty. But I still would hate to have to live like that." He said.

Samuel laughed again. "Let's take a look at their life and yours in that exact moment." He said.

They were coming home from church and the whole family was heading out to watch one of the kids play soccer. The mother, her name is Brandy. She was going on and on about how it was such a good thing that they had not bought that new minivan now they had money to go on a much nicer vacation this year.

You on the other hand were coming from a grocery store having gotten into an argument with your wife. Do you remember? You wanted to grill out steaks and have the neighbors over and she thought you shouldn't spend the money. Do you remember feeling a slight pang of guilt Bob?

You felt that guilt because you don't really like that particular neighbor do you? You thought a few really nice steaks and some expensive wine would show him that you were doing just as well as he was with his fancy new car. But Donna doesn't care about such things."

Bob felt chastised.

He thought back to his life review and how he hadn't really judged himself. Now he was. He was judging himself not for arguing with his wife, not even for his condescending thoughts about strangers in the old station wagon. He judged himself because he knew he was capable of being a much better person.

He started to realize what Samuel was trying to show him.

"Those people in the station wagon probably looked at me and thought, 'there but for the grace of God go I'."

Samuel laughed again. "You're being too hard on yourself Bob. That's not the point.

The point is that God isn't leaving anyone alone. Even in the most extreme circumstance if people ask God will be right next to them. You'd be surprised at what a little faith and wisdom can get you through in life."

A memory flashed in Bob's mind. It was a few years ago but the feeling was that it was happening to him right at the moment. He was standing outside at a flea market on a hot summer day. A friend of Bob's owned a little business selling baseball cards and other collectibles.

He and Bob were chatting when a boy about 12 or 13 walked up to buy a particular baseball card. The boy had these huge lips and bucked teeth. He spoke slowly and with something of a slur. He had old worn tennis shoes on and dirty blue jeans and a t-shirt. His brown hair was combed but clearly not professionally cut. It looked like his mom or dad had last cut it a few months ago and done a bad job.

Next to the boy was a younger boy. Obviously his brother. The younger child looked rather average but also clearly not from a wealthy family or even what Bob would consider middle class kid. The kid kept looking up to the older boy that as he talked about the price of the baseball card.

Bob's friend sensing the kid didn't have a lot of money lowered the price to four dollars and the boy reached into his pocket and pulled out

three dollar bills and a small handful of change. He counted out the change leaving him with just a few pennies. The boy then gave the baseball card to his younger brother who broke out in a huge smile. The goofy looking older brother just stared blankly and they walked away.

He could see the kid so clearly in his mind it was if he was actually standing in front of him. Samuel could see the angst in Bob's face.

"The thing that bugs me" Bob said, "is that it looks like some people never get any kind of break in life. They are born different looking. They have no money and they don't even have very good social skills. It seems like they don't get a real good shot at life."

"You were missing something when you looked at the boy." Samuel said.

Bob was visibly startled that Samuel knew exactly what he was thinking.

"If the boy had been mean would you have remembered him?"

Bob thought for a moment. "I suppose not. I recall that I thought he was such a nice little kid. I remember wondering why such a nice kid had to look the way he did and why he had to be born with such awkward speech and social skills. The only time the kid even smiled was when he first walked up to the table with all of the baseball cards on it. He looked at me and my friend and smiled just slightly. But he didn't really seem happy."

"When you first got here your ego was removed and you were just Bob with your soul and your real self. I am going to show you this young boy as he really is. You will see his soul and the essence of his heart. His entire being and not just his physical shell."

In an instant Bob was back at the flea market. He was standing next to his friend when the young boy walked up. Bob felt his legs go weak. He was staring at the boy but he could see him as God did. He could see him as he wished he could see everyone. The only way he could describe him was that

this young boy was love. He was the purest human being Bob had ever seen.

Bob felt his legs wobble wildly and he fell to the ground sobbing. He could not speak or stop crying.

Then he was back with Samuel and felt the angel's hand on his shoulder. Bob looked up through blurry eyes and finally spoke.

"He is the most beautiful thing I have ever seen."

Samuel looked into Bob's eyes. "Do you understand love better now?" He asked.

"That little boy had a pure love for his little brother. He got more joy out of buying that baseball car for his little brother than most people would get from buying an expensive car for themselves. In fact, that little boy was filled more joy than a billionaire who gives a million dollars to starving children. He knows that he is giving everything he has to his little brother. He knows that he brought joy to his little brother.

The boy with the big teeth will grow into this teeth. The shabby shoes and worn clothes are all that he really needs. He has plans for his future and plans for his little brother's future. He doesn't worry about those plans or the future. Today he has food and he has the love of his brother. He is happy and has no stress. He is enjoying life in a way too many people miss. He is having fun!

Bob was starting to feel comfortable talking with the angel Samuel. Thoughts were racing through his mind and he tried to focus on one particular emotion that was tied to a time in his life. The time when his father had died. Before he could speak he knew that Samuel knew what Bob was thinking. He began to feel the deep despondency he had felt when his father had died. The incredible pain that seemed to be present in every cell of his body.

He looked directly into Samuel's eyes without blinking. Samuel's face was serene. "Why is it so hard?" Bob asked.

Samuel answered with a soft smile. "Would you rather it were easy?"

Bob was startled at the suggestion. This was the second time Samuel had said this and now it was really sinking in. He was starting to understand so clearly the nature of much of his suffering.

He felt pain when his father passed because he loved him so completely. If his father's death had been easy it would have meant that he didn't have that strong bond and that deep love.

He bowed his head and rubbed his hands together lost in thought. Something was still missing. The suffering over loss was easy to understand. But what about the suffering of people who just had more challenging lives? They suffered with things that Bob could never even imagine experiencing.

A flood of thoughts poured into his mind. He could see the images in his head. He saw images of paralyzed children. Grown adults with Down's syndrome, people suffering horribly in concentration camps and many other awful images of abject poverty and suffering that had nothing to do with the loss of a loved one.

Bob hadn't said a word and yet Samuel the angel knew exactly what he was thinking about.

"When you have a relationship with God the pain and the hurt can only go so deep. It can only touch a small part of you. The bigger part of you, your soul, can continue to be joyous right up until the moment you die. And then as you have seen, it gets even better." Samuel said.

Samuel continued.

"All of creation is good. God could put you in a hammock your entire physical life. Nothing would ever happen that was bad or painful. But that is not the point of life. You experience great joy and great sorrow. From both of those things you learn. You also connect to others more.

To be truly connected and to truly love each other requires both the pain and the joy. You learn and grow from both. For most of your life you really haven't experienced pain and suffering. You've had bad times, but they've always been brief and you have rebounded. Until you had your financial troubles you had really never had a long streak of bad things happen to you. How happy were you then?"

This was something that Bob had never considered. As he thought back on his life he realized that Samuel already knew the answer to the question. He also realized how empty his life had been. He and Donna both had been going through the motions of a happy successful life. But to what end? A deep and unsettling sadness came over him.

"I haven't been getting closer to my wife and children. I've been getting further away. That's not right is it?"

"No it isn't." Samuel answered.

"You love your wife and you love your children. But you don't have the deep love and connection that should come with time. If you stay on the path that you are on you will not get closer to them. You will get further away."

Bob begin to see how some of the bad things had actually drawn his family closer together. He and Donna were never closer then when his dad had died. When the kids were sick they also got closer.

"Does God sometimes use pain and suffering to bring us closer together?" He asked.

"Yes." Samuel answered.

"And now you see how well it works. That doesn't mean you should go in search of bad times. Far from it. You should go in search of happiness and joy. You should seek joy, not misery. When the bad times come you must be aware of them and appreciate them for what they are. Then you will find that when others are going through bad things you can reach out honestly to them. You can make new connections and strengthen existing connections.

There is more to it than just a learning experience and a growth experience. You must also understand that God doesn't cause these things to happen. When someone is murdered or killed accidently by the reckless behavior of another it doesn't mean God did this. It means that people have free will and will sometimes do things that hurt others. "

Bob was silent for several minutes. He knew what he wanted to ask. He also knew that he didn't know what exactly to ask. The question that was inside finally came out.

"I understand what you are saying about suffering and the personal side of it. I studied some history in college. How did God let the holocaust happen and how did God let all of those millions of people starve to death in the Ukraine?

I mean, Stalin murdered millions and millions of people by starving them. I understand free will and that Hitler and Stalin had help from other people with free will. But couldn't God stop this? "

Samuel looked intently at Bob and spoke very slowly.

"Do you think it is worse when millions of people are murdered than it is when one person is murdered? Do you think it's worse when one member of a family, a son or a daughter are murdered than when the entire family is murdered?

Each human being is connected to every other human. And every one of you is connected to God and Heaven. We feel it. But you feel it too.

And you feel it not just during the painful times but during the joyous times. You feel it and you know it deep inside of yourself when you look at something beautiful."

Bob was searching his mind. Something was still missing. Something hard to articulate. He put it into words as best he could and hoped Samuel would understand.

"Didn't most people suffer for most of their lives? Five hundred years ago, or even a hundred years ago most people lived in poverty. They didn't have nice homes, or even shabby homes. They lived in dirt huts and caves. They had nothing but work and suffering. Their children often died early, they went hungry and they didn't have any entertainment, happiness or joy in their lives."

"You are trying to put God in a time box." Samuel answered simply

"But I've always heard that God doesn't change." Bob said.

"That means the nature of God, and it's true, God doesn't change. But people do. You are trying to view the universe in terms of just things again. Things that have been invented, new technologies that make your life easier and new medicines that make you healthier. These are wonderful things and they make life easier. But they are not life itself.

If someone from two hundred years ago was revived today, they might think that airplanes, computers, cars, cures for many diseases and even food delivery was somehow magical wouldn't they? So what would they need God for?"

"That is almost exactly what I am trying to ask." Bob answered.

Think about the moment you died and your body was lying on that bed in the hospital. Think about how you were floating above your body and moving through the hospital. Think of how you moved through the universe so quickly. Think about how we have moved around the Earth and

through the city since you have been dead. You just focused on it and there you were transported instantly.

Do you think anything will be invented in the next ten thousand years that will impress you after what you have seen today?"

Bob smile and answered quickly, "No, but those people would not have seen this either unless they went through the same experience that I did."

He was surprised that he had thought of such a good answer so quickly. And then Samuel shot him down.

"So what?" Samuel responded just as quickly.

People hundreds of years ago were concerned about different things. They knew that there were two worlds. They were living on Earth in a physical word. They were not stupid. They tried to make their lives easier on Earth. The idea of having designer shoes and purses was not even a consideration.

They focused on doing what they needed to do to live. But they also focused on doing what they needed to do to get to Heaven. They saw Earth as temporary. Not everyone is like you even today Bob. Some people focus their lives on exploring the Earth. They want to see things and people that interest them.

Others live their lives on helping people, or loving and enjoying their families. It has always been this way. And while people have always just floated through life, it has always been their choice to do so.

Bob felt chastised. He knew Samuel was talking about him and his shoes and the designer purses he had bought for Donna.

You ask why there is suffering, but you didn't ask the other question. Why is there beauty?"

Bob was silent for a moment. He realized he had never questioned why something was beautiful or why the word even existed. A thing was either beautiful or it wasn't. But the more he thought about Samuel's question the more intrigued he became.

"I guess I never even thought about it. I just assumed that some things were beautiful and some were ugly and some things just are. But I do know that some things I look at truly are beautiful. I just don't know why and I don't know why there is such a thing as beauty." He said.

"As a human being, an animal as some people believe, what purpose is there to beauty? Why would it even exist as a notion? The beauty that you see in a painting is the same beauty you will see in music. A popular song that took an hour or two to write and compose may be enjoyable. It may even be functional in that you can dance to it, or tap your foot along to distract your mind. But you would never call it beautiful.

Some songs are beautiful. Some classical symphonies and operas are widely considered not just entertaining, but beautiful. The music has something in common with the paintings. They both require a great deal of work. Now I want to show you something else."

In an instant Bob was standing on a mountain or very high hill. Directly across from his view were two very tall mountains and smaller mountains to the left and right.

The taller mountains were snowcapped and would change in color from a deep blue just below the snow to a charcoal grey, then lighter grey and then blended in with a line of dark green trees. In front of the trees was a vast open field of rolling hills that were a deep and vibrant green. To his left was another line of trees with white trunks and beautiful yellow and gold leaves. Directly in front of him was a still lake that reflected perfectly the beauty surrounding.

"This is perfectly beautiful." Bob said. "Is this in Heaven?

Samuel laughed and shook his head.

"No Bob, this is Switzerland!"

The reason I showed you this is that it also has something in common with the beauty of the paintings and the beauty of the music. This took hard work. It took an attention to detail to make the Earth just as it takes hard work and attention to detail to make beautiful art.

The reason beauty exists, and the reason beauty makes you feel happy is to show you that any work that is creative and constructive builds a beautiful world. It also builds into you a deep respect and appreciation for hard work.

God wants you to understand and appreciate the work that was done to make the Earth and to make it beautiful. If God can make the Earth this beautiful, surely you can work hard enough to make your own little piece of the world beautiful. Then on the days that you rest you are relaxing in the midst of beauty.

You know when you have created something beautiful that you feel good. You also know that you cannot create something beautiful without hard work and focused effort."

"What about when I do bad things? I know that I do them. I know that I shouldn't. I can be very judgmental Samuel. I've read parts of The Bible. I know some of it. But I really don't understand what I'm supposed to do to live a better life. When I'm honest with people I feel better. When I do the right thing I feel happy. Still I really don't know how I am supposed to live. I think that's the problem with a lot of people. We read the bible and it says to repent. But I really don't even know what that means. How should I live my life?"

HOW SHOULD I LIVE MY LIFE?

Repentance is to change the way you think. It just means to turn away from doing the bad things you have done.

Samuel said.

"If you want to know how to live your life, you have to know how to change your life. The only way to change your life is to change the way you think.

"You said when you do the right thing you feel better. You feel happy. Have you ever noticed that this is true even if the right thing hurts you?"

Bob nodded slowly as the realization came over him. "Yes. I can't think of a single time when I did the right thing and felt bad about it. It made whatever problem I was facing smaller."

"So the challenge in your life is to have that feeling all the time. This is where so many people get it wrong. You don't have to suffer and have a life filled with pain to learn and get to Heaven.

As part of every life there will be times when you suffer and you are in pain. If you do the right thing, and you know what that is, you can make it through and still be happy. More importantly you can become a better person. You can help others through bad times and you can bring the divided parts of your life in to a single life. You can bridge your spiritual life and your physical life."

When you read The Bible as a list of commands that make your life harder you are missing the point. This is not the intent. The Bible is your

manual for a happy life with a connection to God. It is necessary for you to understand that it is written to give you peace in your soul. Which means peace very deep down in your mind.

Many read The Bible as a literal word. Sometimes this is true, other times it is not. Still others study The Bible hoping God will talk to them. This is also often true. The Bible is to be both studied and read. It is not easy. It is a deeply intellectual undertaking. Think of the story of David. He sleeps with his friend's wife. Rather than face the consequences he has his friend killed. There is much to that story. David did the logical thing by killing his friend. For David it got rid of a problem. That's the point of many of the stories of The Bible. The logical solution is often evil. But that doesn't mean it's the right decision. The Bible can help you to live your life and stay connected to God.

When you try to live life connected to God and become as what you would call a 'good' person you will not only feel better and be happier, you bring Heaven to Earth."

"When I do go to church, and I know I don't go every Sunday, I get confused about what I am supposed to do. I really have tried to follow the commandments and I used to pray, but it never seemed to work. Look at all of the bad things that have happened to me over the last few years. I don't think any of my prayers were answered," Bob said.

Samuel laughed heartily. "Of course they were answered," He thundered.

"You were praying for relief and peace. You thought you were praying for more money, but you were actually praying not to worry about money as much. I know some of the things that happened weren't about money. When a child gets sick you prayed only for the health. That prayer was answered.

This isn't true for everyone. Some people who are very good and loving lose children to horrible diseases and violence at the hands of

others. These children aren't complaining in Heaven. Have you not noticed many of them don't even complain on Earth? Their eyes are open. They may just be open only a little bit to the great things that are coming, but they are open.

They know all pain and suffering is temporary. You spent most of your prayers asking for money. Asking for a better job, a bigger house or a nicer car. The thing you really wanted was to have all of these things and not the stress of having to work for them or worry over them. What you really wanted was peace.

You also missed the fact that once you thought you were going to make more money you started to feel more stress. You were focused on getting new stuff. But you were blind to the fact that the focus on the material is what was taking your peace from you.

You were also taking the peace from your wife and children. You stressed over unimportant things that you wanted. They felt that stress. Your children learn from you and you taught them that without a big home and a fancy car they should have stress.

God did not cause you to lose your job. When it happened he answered your prayers and showed you that much of your anguish was caused by wanting things that were not making you happy. Now you see that it wasn't just your prayers that were answered. Others were praying for you. They were praying you would be happy, and you were! Then when you thought you could go back to your old life you were becoming unhappy again."

Bob smiled. "So how do I get this feeling all the time? What do I have to do to repent? I guess I'm asking what my penance is or how do I get on the right track so I'm happy all of the time?

"You think repentance is something that is hard and will make your life worse. It makes your life better. It makes you happy to think differently." Samuel answered.

"You need to get the vision out of your mind. The vision of some old preacher holding up The Bible and yelling 'Repent you foul sinner!'

In that vision, a man, not God, is standing over you and you feel as if he is going to smack you on the head with The Bible. That's not how it works and not how you should live your life.

The guilt and anguish you feel over doing something wrong aren't just an indicator that you've made a bad choice. Those feelings are also a punishment. You don't want to feel that way all the time so you are chastised.

God is present in your life but he isn't going to reward you for doing bad things. Do you reward your children when they do something bad? Do you think that would be good for your children? Of course not.

If you want to stop feeling bad about the things you have done, stop doing bad things. That sounds really easy doesn't Bob?"

"Yes it does. But it isn't." Bob answered.

"No it isn't. It takes time and practice just like everything else. Repenting from your sins means turning away from them. It means not to let bad thoughts fester in your mind. You don't need a preacher hammering you to do that. To do that, you have to focus on good things. You have to focus on what is right and honorable.

When you do that the guilt, remorse and anguish begin to fade. Then you will begin to be much happier. You'll also find that you don't need to get your happiness from external things. When you get your joy from people it lasts much longer."

Bob lowered his head. He was embarrassed and unsure how to ask the important question.

"Look Samuel; I have to be honest with you. I've been to church before and maybe I just didn't pay attention, but I still don't know how to

do this. I don't know how to change the way I think and I don't know what to think about. I understand that I need to change my thinking, but I have no idea how to go about it."

"Most people don't." Samuel said.

"The first thing you must do is to have time alone. Just a few minutes every day to start. If you are in your car, turn off the radio. If you are at home, turn off the television and any other distractions. Then just sit quietly and think about your place in the universe.

These days too many people think of themselves as a little speck of sand in this vast universe. They think of themselves as small and insignificant. If you are so small and the universe is so big how can your life have meaning? Bob, you are the meaning. You are intricately and permanently connected to the entire universe.

When you focus on that connection you can begin to feel it. The easiest and most obvious connection is to God, who created all of this, and to each other.

Lay down and be still for a second."

Bob realized that there was a soft mattress suddenly behind him. He lay back and was instantly relaxed. He was completely alone.

Samuel, the angel guiding him had vanished. He could see stars, galaxies, planets and even landscapes. Some were pastoral settings with lush green fields and flowers that were so vibrant and beautifully colored that they could not exist on earth. Other landscapes looked like large cities made of light.

He could see the earth as well. He was aware of people moving through the landscapes and the earth. He saw animals and plants and everything on the earth and everything in the heavenly landscapes and the universe itself.

Then he was aware of his connection to all of the things he was seeing. A brilliant gold light emanated from his body out towards every single thing that he could see. As the light got further from him and closer to other people, plants, animals and even entire stars he could see the light was actually made from strings of golden thread.

The objects he was connected to were shooting out golden threads to every other object. The entire universe was connected by these beautiful strings that appeared to vibrate. He noticed the most beautiful music he had ever heard. It played softly as he absorbed all of the different connections and the meaning of those threads.

A profound realization came over him. As soon as it started, it ended and he was sitting up facing Samuel again.

"Now do you see?" Samuel asked.

"Yes." Bob answered.

"It's not that I'm part of the universe or connected to the universe. We are the universe. It is all one thing. It is one massive creation."

Samuel nodded and smiled.

"That is what you need to understand when you repent. When you repent you are thinking about the good things. You are thinking about the love that you have not just for your family and friends, but for everything that has been created.

When you focus on the creation and your connection to everything it becomes much easier to think good thoughts and to turn your mind to love. Suffering for the things you have done is not repentance. Repenting doesn't cause sadness, anguish and misery. Repenting leads to joy.

When you focus your eyes on something you can move your body to what you are focusing on. Your mind works the same way. If you focus your

mind on getting things you will be successful. But it is better to focus your mind on doing things and thinking about your life.

When I tell you to think about your life I mean it. Think about your life, not what you are going to do with your life.

Focus on yourself as a person. That person is connected to other people. Think about that more than what you want to get, or do in the future. Think bigger than just the things, think about the life. When you do that you have a goal that will outlast any problem and outrun any gain.

If you keep thinking about your life as a collection of things that you have you will be greatly disappointed every time the list doesn't grow.

If you keep hitting yourself in the head with a hammer, that will cause pain. Repent! Stop doing that and stop thinking about it all the time. Instead, think about the things I have told you. Think about loving other people. Then you will want to encourage and help them to be happy.

On the other hand, if you live your life hating a group of people because of how much money they make, or where they live, or the color of their skin, how will you ever be happy? How will you be able to go to Heaven where there are even more different people?

You have a wonderful chance to make this earth like Heaven. You will never fully succeed. But you can make it wonderful. You can make it better. You can work to make earth more like Heaven. Live and function on the earth, but keep your mind on Heaven.

Bob knew that Samuel was finished. This last message was important and he would learn no more.

"Am I going back now?" Bob asked.

"Yes. But before you do I must tell you one last thing. Not everything you have learned will you remember. Some of it will be at the back of your mind but you will not be able to articulate the thought. It will be there to

guide you. The experience you will remember. The love and the feeling of being connected you will also remember.

You must not dwell on it too much. You are on the Earth and you are going back to live in your physical body. In the first months there will be pain from your accident. Do not dwell on that pain. You will be coming back to Heaven, but it will be a long time. So you must live your life as I have told you. On Earth, but connected to God."

Bob began to understand. The things he felt inside that were missing and how to live his life. He understood that free will is much like freedom on earth. He cannot have dignity without freedom. He cannot have dignity without free will. He must have courage which means integrity. He must have character to do the things he says he will do and he must have honor to exercise his free will and do the right thing. People must reconnect both the physical and spiritual lives to accomplish these things. Then even in bad times he will have happiness in his life.

The single most important thing is to keep good thoughts in your mind and keep bad thoughts out. You live on this earth.

He knew he had to go back and he was excited. But he also knew that if he stayed here everything would be fine with his family. And he really wanted to stay.

Samuel knew what Bob was thinking.

"You have to go back Bob."

BACK TO LIFE

The moment Samuel finished his sentence Bob felt himself moving through space again. He knew he was going back. He wanted to protest. He wanted to stay, but it was too late. Bob was moving through space again. This time he had the feeling he was falling.

There were no beautiful golden lights and there was no music or soft sounds. It was just an irritating buzzing. He saw his body lying on the hospital bed. He lost consciousness.

He was back in his body. The first sensation when he tried to open his eyes was pain. His chest hurt the worst but he was aware of pain in his leg and his ribs. His eyes were closed but he could sense someone standing over him. He could not speak. There was a large plastic tube snaked down his throat. He started to gag. He could hear the buzzing of machines in the room and feel the air going through the tube and into his lungs.

The person standing over him moved around in a blur checking him and the machines. It was a nurse or doctor he didn't know. He could vaguely tell that it appeared to be a young man. After checking everything the man leaned over Bob to fiddle with the IV tube going into his arm.

"Hang in there partner." The man said. "You're doing really great. I'm giving you a little more pain medication and soon we'll take that breathing tube out and you'll feel much more comfortable."

Bob tried to smile at the man but quickly fell back to sleep.

When he woke again he realized the breathing tube was gone. He opened his eyes and tried to process his surroundings. The pain in his chest was dull. He knew he was in a hospital but couldn't remember how he got there.

He struggled to keep his eyes open expecting to see a doctor or his wife Donna. As his eyes focused he realized the man standing over him was Tom Lawson, his coworker. The man Bob had kept his distance from because he thought he was to "churchy".

Bob tried to smile but the pain gripped him and he grimaced.

"Tom, what are you doing here?"

Tom smiled down at him. Bob couldn't help but feel a stronger connection to the man. He didn't know why he was here. He really didn't know Tom all that well, but did know that Tom was a very good man.

"I was not far behind you when you had the accident. I called the office and got your home phone number so that I could call your wife. She just stepped outside, I'll go get her."

Bob closed his eyes and started to drift off to sleep again when he heard the door to his room swing open. Donna still had the marks from tears and mascara running down her face. But she was smiling now.

"Bob I thought you were dead." She cried.

Bob tried to muster a smile but the pain was bearing down on him. "I'm okay sweetie, it just hurts a lot, but I think I'm okay. Where are the kids?"

"My mom has them. As soon as Tom called I called her and left them at the neighbors so I could get here right away.

She was leaning over his face and stroking his head, unsure how to touch him and how badly he was hurt. The doctor told her that they had lost him for a brief moment and she decided to tell Bob.

"The doctor said your heart stopped for a second. Can you believe that? You were actually dead for a minute or two. He said once they got a little

tear in your aorta fixed that you came right back and that you should be fine. It was scary though because all this happened so fast.

Tom told me it looked like you were still awake and talking when he saw them put you in the ambulance. He said it looked like a bad accident but it looked like you were doing okay and I shouldn't worry.

He is such a nice guy Bobby. Why didn't you tell me what good friends you two were? I've never even met him."

Bob tried to focus on her question about Tom but he was too confused. He was sure he had been out for days but Donna said his heart only stopped for a minute or two. Maybe he had been in a coma for all this time that he had been in Heaven. It had to have been at least a few days. He couldn't remember sleeping. He remembered seeing Heaven, or that city outside Heaven and talking to Samuel.

He needed to know what day it was. He needed to know how long he had been in a coma. It could have been days or even weeks. How much of his life had he missed?

"What day is this?" He asked.

Donna had a confused look on her face. She wiped a strand of brown hair away from her eyes.

"It's still Friday. It's almost Eleven O'clock though. You've been out for a couple of hours. Do you want me to see if I can get you something to eat or drink?"

"You mean I've only been here for six hours? Didn't I have work today? I know I went to work this morning. Did I have a heart attack? Has Tom been here this entire time? I thought I had been here for days."

The confusion was beginning to overwhelm him.

"You are just so tired sweetie. Just rest. I'll get you something to drink."

Bob looked up at his wife. He had a funny thought about the day they got married and he could see her standing at the altar. He wondered why he thought of that at this moment and started to feel a flood of thoughts coming back to his mind. He remembered Samuel. He started to think he must have had a really crazy dream and let himself slip back into sleep.

When he opened his eyes again he knew it was morning. The sun was shining through the single window to his right. He was alone in his hospital room.

The pain was dull and making him uncomfortable. He tried to raise his head but this made the pain rocket through his entire body. He looked around moving his head as little as possible. He knew he had survived something and he had a fleeting thought that there had been a car accident. His mind was too fuzzy to remember anything clearly. He had thoughts about the dream he had had as well. And yet something in the back of his mind was telling him to hold on to that. To hold on to those memories because it hadn't been a dream.

Over the next couple of days the pain began to subside. He slept most of the time and in the short moments he was awake he talked to Donna about the accident. He would be getting out of the hospital by the end of the week but he was told that his recovery might take some time.

Tom Lawson had stopped by to see him again on Monday after work, but other than that he had no other visitors from the office. The executive team had sent flowers with a card that said get well soon. As far as his job was concerned and his new promotion he hadn't heard anything. He had tried to talk to Donna about it but she had told him not to worry and that he needed to rest.

On Friday morning they took his leg out of the traction and let him move around in a wheel chair. All of the tubes had been pulled and the pain

killers were now just pills that he could take when he needed them. So far he had taken none. He decided a clearer head was preferable to the pain.

He was released from the hospital Friday afternoon just one week after the accident. It was great to be back and see the kids. But he mostly slept.

On Saturday the pain was bad and he slept all day, but on Sunday things began to feel much better. His new boss Roger Davidson had called and wanted to stop by the house for a visit on Monday.

So when Monday came Bob was ready. He hadn't taken any pain medication so his mind was clear. Donna had helped him get comfortably seated in a chair in the living room and Bob had even managed to dress somewhat professionally. They had just cut a leg out of a pair of pants above the knee to allow for the cast.

When Roger showed up at about three in the afternoon Bob was feeling pretty good. He knew he had a few months of rehab in front of him but his doctor had said he could get back to work on a limited schedule in just three more weeks if all went well. The rehab would cause him to lose just a few hours twice every week for a few months. They really couldn't be any more specific about the timing because his lower leg had been so badly broken.

When he told his boss the news he saw the man's face change.

"Hey Bob, we're all real happy that you are pulling through this. We really are. You are such a vital part of the organization and have done such a great job."

When he hesitated after the last sentence Bob knew there was trouble.

"The thing is, as you know we are kind of short on leadership right now. So what we are going to do is put the director position on hold for just a little while and give it to Tom Lawson and then we'll get you all lined up for the next spot."

Bob was shocked at himself with his response.

"Roger, don't worry about a thing. I'm sure you guys are just doing what you think is best for the company and I'll be okay no matter what happens,"

Roger was even more shocked than Bob. He knew Bob to be a go getter and a fighter and had expected a bit of a battle. He tried to remain professional as he said his good bye. After he left Bob hobbled into the kitchen to talk to Donna.

"Well, the promotion is off but at least I still have my job. Donna had known Bob for years and was waiting for the blow up. She knew he would be irate.

"Oh Bobby, I'm so sorry, I knew everything will work out." She offered.

Bob smiled a bit and just nodded. He was feeling tired and asked her for help in getting back into bed. While he lay with his eyes open he found himself straining to be upset. He wanted to stew on this bad news.

It didn't come easily. For some reason he felt different about things. He knew everything was going to be okay. He started to think about Tom Lawson. He focused what anger he could muster on Tom. He called Donna into the bedroom.

"Honey I finally figured out why Tom visited me so often when I was in the hospital."

"Oh?"

"He was checking to see if I could come back to work. I'm sure Tom fed Roger and the others a bunch of info about my health and told them it would be a long time before I could be back at work. He was the second choice and he is the one who got the job. Worked out pretty perfectly for old Tom didn't it?"

Donna looked confused. "I'm not so sure about that Bobby. He seemed to be genuinely concerned about you. Did you know he also brought dinner to me and the kids Sunday night?"

"Oh? I didn't know that. Maybe he was just fishing for more information. Sometimes those real religious guys are just putting on a show. That's how they lure you in to trusting them. Then they hit you broadside."

"Well you know him better than I do. It's too bad because I really thought he was a nice guy."

Bob finally fell asleep after starting at the ceiling for a good half hour. He was starting to remember his experience much more clearly. He wanted to take another pain pill to dull the physical pain and fog his mind a bit. He just didn't want the work of concentrating on what had happened to him.

After an hour of fitful sleep Donna woke him up.

"Bobby, Tom Lawson just called. He asked if he could come over and see you. I didn't want to wake you before but I told him it would be okay. Is that okay or do you want me to try and call him back and just tell him you are sleeping?"

"Now what the hell does he want?" Bob said.

"He's got the job. No need for any more shows."

Donna just shrugged her shoulders.

"Well, maybe he has a few questions about my clients. I don't know. I guess we'll find out.

He mustered a small smile and pulled himself out of the bed and back to the living room chair. He flipped the television on and tried to clear his mind by watching old reruns. His mind was moving back to the angel

Samuel. He began to realize that those fleeting thoughts were starting to come together very clearly.

It hadn't been any dream. He had certainly never had a dream like that. He had heard about people having near death experiences and he tried to remember what they had said. Was his experience like the others? He started to feel very good about life and himself and the doorbell rang. It was Tom Lawson and it snapped him back to the problem at hand.

Tom rushed in quickly so Bob didn't have to get up. He stood over the chair and shook Bob's hand.

"You look great! I can't believe how much better you've gotten and how fast. Are you in pain?"

Bob faked a smile. "Thanks Tom. It's not too bad. They gave me something or other to take but it kind of makes my brain fuzzy so I've just been working through it. It's really much better than it was a few days ago. I'll tell you that. And hey, thanks for getting dinner for Donna and the kids last Sunday. She really appreciated it and I know it helped."

"Oh hey, no problem at all. I'm sorry I couldn't do more. I really am. I know how hard something like this can be on the whole family and if there is anything else I can do please just ask."

"Thanks Tom, I sure will." Bob wished Tom would get to the point. He wanted to know about how he got his promotion and why he was here. Tom wouldn't bring it up.

"Bob I mean that." Tom continued

"I want you to call me if there is something I can do. I know people say that all of the time and don't mean it. Or they do and for some reason people won't ask for the help. Really, I want to help and I've got some free time."

Free time? That threw Bob for a loop. He had just gotten a promotion. How was he going to have free time?

"I don't know about free time Tom. Roger was just here a few hours ago and told me they gave you the promotion. I guess I kind of understand. I mean, as you know it might be as long as six months before I'm completely back to normal."

"Six months?" Tom gasped. "Wow! I thought there would be some rehab but I told the guys at work I thought you would be back in full force in just a week or two. I guess I was being too optimistic."

Bob was becoming more confused by the second. Maybe Donna was right. It sure did seem like Tom really was the genuine article, but it still didn't explain the free time.

"Well, since you're the new Midwest sales director, aren't you going to be pretty busy?"

"Actually Bob I resigned today. So I don't know if Roger is going to be calling you again later or if they are going to offer the job to someone else. I'm sorry. I guess I should have asked so I could tell you."

"Wait a second. You resigned? I mean, you just quit? Why?" Bob said.

"I know I make you uncomfortable some times when I pray at lunch, and I'm sorry about that, let's just say I think I have a different calling for my life." Tom said.

"You didn't make me uncomfortable at lunch when you prayed. I guess it's just not something I do, but I was fine with you praying. Sorry if I made you feel that way." Bob said.

"It's okay Bob. Religion isn't for everyone, and even though I know I'm seen as 'that religious guy' at work the truth is I've gone to five different churches in the last couple of years. Something deep inside me is telling me

that I need to start my own church. I actually had a minor in theology in college and I've just decided I really want to do this.

So, that's the bigger reason I quit. I want to be a preacher. Probably sounds kind of crazy doesn't it?"

Bob was speechless. The experience he had was now flooding back to him in crystal clear detail. It was as if it had happened this morning. He could see Samuel clearly. He could remember the things he had learned.

He was at a fork in the rode of his life. He knew exactly what he was supposed to do. But old feelings were creeping in to his mind.

What would he do about money? How would he pay the house payment? What if he was back in line for the promotion?

His headed started to hurt. He was struggling with a thought. Why wasn't he happier about this? Was it because he was still unsure about the promotion? He closed his eyes and rubbed at his temples. He had been wrong about Tom, and that had turned out to be good, because now he was back in the hunt for the promotion. Yet something was bothering him. What was it? Why was he so confused?

"You okay Bob?"

The sound of Tom's voice startled him.

"Oh. Yeah I'm okay. My head is just hurting a bit."

"Well, I'd better get going. You need your rest and I want to get home and celebrate with my wife and kids anyway. "

Bob nodded politely. Something was troubling him and he found it hard to articulate without sounding like a jerk.

"Tom, why did you come here to tell me this?"

He could see the surprise in Tom's face.

"To be completely honest Bob, I'm not sure. I did want to check on you and see how you were doing. I also wanted to tell you I wasn't take the director job. The real reason? I'm not sure. Something inside me was telling me to go see you and tell you why I was quitting and what I was going to do. It probably sounds crazy, but something just kept telling me I should talk to you."

Bob just stared at him and said, "I really don't think it sounds crazy at all Tom."

The two sat in silence neither knowing quite what to day next. Tom finally stood and left awkwardly.

Before he left he handed Bob a piece of paper with his phone number on it and told him once again to call if he or Donna needed anything at all.

Bob fell asleep in the chair. He was mentally exhausted. After an hour or so Donna gently nudged him awake.

"Bobby you should go back to bed."

He opened his eyes and looked at her beautiful face. He loved his wife. He knew it with every fiber of his being. He knew what it was to love with his soul now. He also knew how lucky he was to have met her and married her. It would all start with her.

"Sit down for a second sweetie. I want to tell you something. Remember when I came to in the hospital and you said my heart had stopped for a minute?"

Donna nodded. A worried look on her face. "Yes, I remember."

"I died Donna. I died and I saw Heaven."

She tilted her head and looked into his eyes. "What?"

"I saw Heaven. I saw angels, I saw my dad, grandparents and other people I didn't even know I knew. I met an angel named Samuel."

He was getting excited. The feelings of joy were starting to flood back over him.

Tears were starting to form in the corner of Donna's eyes. She was smiling and crying.

They never talked about religion, their faith or God. He knew that she was faithful and deeply spiritual. She just didn't talk about it. She lived it.

"What is it like?" Donna asked.

"The beauty of it is indescribable. The feeling of love is also... indescribable."

He laughed out loud.

"I just... the words are hard to find. It is more than wonderful. It is more than glorious. Those words are not enough to describe it. I could never do it justice. I know you think I was gone only for a minute, but I was there I think for a very long time. It's very hard to explain but time doesn't exist there.

When I talked to the angel we went all over the world. We talked for what had to have been hours and hours, if not days. And yet it all seemed to happen so fast. It seems to have happened in just an instant.

I learned many different things. The most important thing I learned is that we aren't doing this right. Or at least I'm not. I'm not living my life the right way. We are here not to suffer. We are here to love and enjoy life. We are here to make it better. We are here to learn and prepare."

They talked for hours. Bob told Donna all that he had learned and seen. The more he talked the more he could remember. He answered every question she had without having to think about an answer. It all came perfectly back to his mind.

When he had finished he could tell Donna was exhausted. She had been listening so intently to every word he said. She interrupted only once or twice to ask about a detail. She was in awe.

"What are you going to do now?" She asked.

There was no worry at all in her voice. She asked the question with great anticipation and excitement.

"I'm not sure dear, but I think it's going to involve Tom Lawson and I think our lives are going to change for the better."

TRANSITION TO A BETTER LIFE

The next day Roger Davidson had returned. Now Bob had his promotion again. He would work from home when he needed to but told Roger he would be back in the office quickly. He had called him "Killer".

Usually when one of the executives called Bob "Killer" he had smiled. The "Killer" would get the deal. The "Killer" worked hard and knew what he was doing. The "Killer" was ruthless and was getting the promotion. But when Roger called him Killer this time, he felt pain.

For the next three days he slept, ate and thought about his life. He also thought about Samuel and his trip.

The doubts were gone. He knew it was real. It had all been real. He had died and gone to Heaven. He had learned things he could not unlearn or forget. He had been doing it wrong. "It" was everything. He had been living his life the wrong way.

Now, for the first time, he was going to live his life right.

He was going to be happy. He was going to make other people happy and he was going to make the world better.

But how? How was he going to get over the fear? Standing in front of people and trying to sell them pump motors was easy compared to this.

He was going to have to talk about God. He was going to have to talk about Heaven. He was going to have to tell people what had happened to him.

They were going to think he was crazy. He knew it. He had seen how people had snickered about Tom Lawson behind his back. This was going to be much worse.

A man has to earn a living. He has to provide for his family. So how was he going to work and make his money and at the same time spread this message? Samuel had told him that he was learning this for a reason. He was allowed to stay longer and remember more than some of the others who had seen it. But that carried a responsibility. He had to spread this message. This truth about life.

He had to start soon. He had to get back to work, and on the first day seize the opportunity to tell his coworkers what he had seen.

_

It was early Monday afternoon. Bob was having his first lunch meeting as a director.

Lunch with the executives had started awkwardly. The crutches made it hard to get around and people kept having to help him. Bob felt a little embarrassed. But the embarrassment was over shadowed by the fear. He could feel it stirring. This lunch was going to be the start of it all. This would be his first step.

David McCarron, the President of the company opened the way. They had just finished ordering when he looked at Bob. "Hey Tom Lawson said your heart actually stopped when you were on the operating table. Is that true?"

Before answering Bob felt a comfort come over his entire body. Of course Tom Lawson would be involved. Of course he would, even though he wasn't here, he was somehow there to help Bob to get started.

"Yeah it sure did David. They tell me it stopped for just minute and half or so, but it felt like it had stopped for days."

"Really? How so? McCarron asked.

"Well, when I was dead I went to Heaven." Bob answered just as a matter of fact. He could feel his muscles tightening. He was getting nervous. Maybe this wasn't the right time. Maybe he should go a bit slower.

"Here we go! You're not going to turn into another Tom Lawson are you?"

It was Roger Davidson. He was laughing at he said it but Bob thought he felt a slight nudge on his leg under the table.

With just the slightest wave of his hand McCarron stopped Roger from talking. He was a man that commanded respect not just from his title as President, but in the way he carried himself.

"I've heard about this kind of thing before. I watched a television show about it years ago. They're called Near Death Experiences aren't they?"

Bob told the men at the table everything. McCarron was interested and hung on his words. When he had finished relating his experience he looked directly at Roger Davidson.

"I may not turn in to another Tom Lawson." He said. "But I'm sure going to try."

"Well, he certainly is a good man." Davidson answered.

"Yes he is." McCarron added.

When the meeting was over Bob returned to his office and closed the door. He picked up the phone and called Tom Lawson at home.

He knew what he was supposed to do. He wanted to be Tom's assistant. He knew it with every fiber of his body.

When Tom answered the phone Bob didn't even say hello. He just started talking.

"Tom, you're going to need help. Every church I think has to have an associate or assistant preacher. You'll have to teach me a lot. When I was in the hospital my heart stopped and I died for a minute. When I did, I saw Heaven, or at least the waiting room for Heaven. I also met an angel names Samuel. He taught me a lot. If you'll have me, I'd like to work for you in your new church."

Tom was taken aback.

"Are you sure about this Bob? I mean, this is a big step. I have money to buy the building and enough to keep us going for no more than a year at best. I would love to have you and I'm really interested in your... experience I guess you would call it? I have to say, I really didn't even think you liked me."

"Tom, sometimes you have to stop hitting yourself in the head with a hammer. Could we meet for dinner on Wednesday?"

JIM STAHLHABER

Eight weeks ago.

* * *

Stahlhaber slammed the phone down. "So where in the hell is Bob Fisher!" He screamed.

There were three other people in his office and his yelling was aimed at no one in particular.

"I've tried calling that guy all day and he hasn't returned my call. Gibbon didn't you tell me we needed those motors by early next week?"

Peter Gibbon, like just about everyone else at Stahlhaber Aerospace, didn't like Jim Stahlhaber. He knew if he didn't give the right answer he would be the object of the wrath.

"Yeah Jim we need them by Wednesday. I talked to Fisher early in the week and he said they would be here either late this week or early next week. We should be fine."

"Dammit Peter you told me yesterday you needed them this week! I've spent that last two hours trying to get Fisher on the phone and now you tell me you don't need them until next week! Do you think I have nothing better to do than babysit you and Bob Fisher all day?!!"

For once Peter decided to stand his ground. He'd seen others do it occasionally and usually Stahlhaber backed down a little.

"Sorry Jim, I was certain I told you yesterday that Bob told me they would be in time for us to start installing them next week and maybe even be here this week."

Jim eyed Peter suspiciously, then thought it wasn't worth the fight. Peter Gibbon was in a good marriage with two young daughters. He had just purchased a new house and his wife didn't work. Jim owned Peter and Peter knew it. Guys like him were nothing but work sheep. They were afraid of life, afraid of losing what little they had. If you gave nice guys like Pete even the smallest amount of respect they might think they could pull one over on you. The guys that were afraid were often his most productive. But they had to be beaten down. You had to treat them like rented mules.

"Okay Pete."

With that everyone left Jim's office. He finally had a few minutes of silence. He didn't feel bad at all about yelling at young Peter Gibbon. You had to let your employees know who was in charge.

He sat back in his chair and picked up the phone to check with his secretary again. Then he decided against it. His secretary was a 26 year old girl named Lexi that he had slept with a year ago. She was drop dead gorgeous.

At the time he was still married. So instead of breaking it off with her and risking her telling Olivia, he did what he always did, offered her a job at too high a salary and then told her he couldn't date her anymore because they were co-workers.

It had always worked in the past. The girls thought they had some great career now and left him alone. A few months later they all quit. Not this Lexi girl, she had stayed. She wouldn't quit. So he was stuck paying her about twice what any other girl would have cost him.

This time it would be okay. Sales had been up this year. Only slightly, but they went from forty million to forty two million dollars. Since he had

inherited the company from his father eight years ago sales had been down every year. But this year they went up.

When he and Olivia had finalized the divorce it had cost him two million in cash. That left him with just under on million dollars in the bank. Now he was done with her. He had to pay child support, but that was peanuts. And his youngest kid was fourteen now, so he only had to pay the twenty grand per month for four more years.

He wanted to pick up the phone just to flirt with Lexi. He had a date tonight with another girl, but maybe he could squeeze in dinner and a little fun with Lexi and then hit the second date around nine. He put the phone back down. If he slept with her again she would have something on him. Better to let this one go. He turned his chair around and stared out the window.

His ex-wife had called earlier. They had been divorced for a few months now and she had mostly left him alone. His oldest son had just gotten into some honors program at school and she just wanted him to call Kyle and congratulate him.

He could feel the stress starting to build. He needed a drink badly. The success of the last year had sparked a little interest from potential buyers. He could dump this business and retire at 48 years old a multi-millionaire.

He tried to entertain the notion. Tried to convince himself that he could sell the business. He could not and he knew it. If he wasn't the President of Stahlhaber Aerospace who was he?

His father was dead. His mother, though only 72 years old was in a full time care facility. Dementia had taken her mind before his dad had passed. His brother and sisters rarely spoke to him. He sent them their ten percent dividend checks like clockwork every quarter. They never thanked him. They never even called to ask how he was doing after the divorce.

He had no one. He liked it that way. He was this business. As much as he hated it, it was who he was.

The world needed people like him and he knew it. When he pulled up to work in a new Ferrari the employees got mad and jealous. But it also motivated them.

For years he would get mad. Really mad. If sales were down his face would turn red, his chest would tighten and he would explode. If they missed a big shipment to a customer the same thing would happen. If a vendor like Bob Fisher was late on a shipment he would blow up.

Now all was good. And yet he was boiling mad inside. The sales staff had been patting themselves on the back like they had done something. Yes, they had increased sales. But that was only because he, Jim Stahlhaber, had whipped them in to shape.

Olivia was no better. She called him every few weeks to tell him something about the kids. But it always involved something he had to do. Call a kid and tell him good job. Go to Andrea's play or concert at school. Why? Why did Olivia continue to bug him about this stuff? It was trivial.

He had come clean about the affairs and asked her for the divorce. She had wanted counseling and said they could work through it. But he know better. It wasn't going to stop any more than the drinking was going to stop.

He had done right by her. Set her up with the house and a wad of cash. But could she leave him alone? Of course not.

The rage was building. There were so many things flipping through his mind. He turned his chair around and started to stand up. Somebody was going to get a little hell today. It would make him feel better and it would keep the workers working hard.

He stopped suddenly. He leaned over and put both hands on the top of the desk to brace himself. Something didn't feel right. He looked from side

to side trying to clear his head. He was sweating. He reached up to wipe the sweat from his brow with one hand. It was slick. He ran his hands through his hair. His entire head was soaked. A small tightness in his chest was getting worse. He slumped back in to his chair and loosened his tie. Now it felt like someone was standing on his chest and his left arm began to feel numb.

"Oh no." He said aloud.

He managed to reach forward to push the button to page Lexi at her desk.

"Yes Mr. Stahlhaber."

"Lexi, I'm having a heart attack. Call an ambulance."

Lexi at first didn't believe him. "Is this a joke Jim?"

But there was no answer. Jim Stahlhaber fell forward on his desk.

JIM IS IN HELL

Jim was floating above his body. He looked down and could himself slumped over his desk. Lexi and others were rushing in to the office. Peter Gibbon, the man he had just berated moments ago was leaning him back into his chair. Jim was oddly detached. He felt no emotion at all.

He looked around his office. He looked around the building. He could see people doing their jobs. He could see people walking in the hallways. Life was going on just a few feet away as if nothing had happened. But he knew clearly that he was dead. It made no difference to him. He was completely detached.

He started to move up. He was floating faster and further from his body. And then he could see nothing. Darkness was all around him. There was a slight buzzing in his ears. He could hear it but it seemed to come from all directions. The faintest of lights was off in the distance. It was a small blue dot. It was bright but seemed very far away. He started to move towards it and the light grew.

After a few seconds two people were next to him. They were smiling at him. One began to speak. "Hey come on Jim. Come with us Jim we'll take care of you."

He ignored them as he slowly moved towards the blue light. The beings next to him were becoming more persistent. "Come on Jim, it's fun here, come with us."

He stopped and looked at them. They were smiling but their smiles weren't real.

He looked at the gold light. It was beginning to get bigger. He knew what it was and he knew where it went.

He slowly moved towards it a little closer.

He knew he didn't belong in that light.

There was no fight in him. He felt himself being pulled down and away from the light.

And then he was in an empty building. The two spirits were gone. He thought it might be a school he had gone to when he was very young. It was one of his first memories of fear. Being in school away from his home and parents had been the first time he could remember being afraid.

The walls were a pale green. He was standing alone looking down a long hallway. The light was dim. Just bright enough to make out the green walls, the gray tile of the floor and doors along each side.

He could sense evil. He had never been more frightened. The fear paralyzed him. And yet he could see nothing but an empty building. The evil presence was behind him. He could sense the horror.

He stood straight with his legs shoulder width apart staring ahead. His hands at his sides straight and tense. He did not want to make a sound. He did not want to move a muscle. He did not want to look behind him.

In an instant his entire body was turned around. The position of his feet did not change. It was as if the building had rotated around him. He closed his eyes not wanting to see the evil now in front of him. He stood for a very long time. When he could think of no other option he slowly opened his eyes.

It was a simple brown door. In the upper center of the door was a window but it was dark glass and he could not see through.

The fear continued to build in him. Something was here. Without moving his head at all he slowly moved his eyes from left to right. There was nothing but the pale green walls on either side of the door.

He could not process any thought or emotion other than a primal fear. It built up inside him until he nearly burst into tears. But he did not know how to get help. He did not know who to call, or where to go. The only thing he could process beyond the fear was that he was completely alone with this evil.

And then he was falling. He fell so fast that his clothes were pulled from his body. He felt a vacuum pulling on him faster and further down. He was sure the vacuum was pulling the cells from his body. He was being pulled through dirt and rock. There were small gaps where he would fall more freely.

The fear was now joined with an anxiety he could not have imagined. As he moved ever downward he could feel his body shaking. He fell hard on the ground. Briefly disoriented the first thing he noticed was the smell. It seeped into his body. A smell of human feces and burning flesh. He heard screams. Faint and lonely at first, but they began to get louder and more numerous. He put his right hand down to lift himself up. His hand grabbed an oddly shaped rock. He looked down to see that it was not a rock but a human skull. He scrambled quickly to his feet and looked around him. The ground was covered with human bones.

His senses now alert, he quickly glanced from spot to spot in his field of vision. It was dark but he could still see clearly. The ground around him was bubbling. At first he thought it was lava. But when he looked closer he could see that it was excrement and flesh oozing out of the ground.

He was aware of the heat. The bubbling cauldron of sewage and flesh was glowing red. There was heat coming from somewhere. Intense heat. The physical anguish had temporarily dulled the fear. The heat and the smell had allowed his mind to focus on something other than the fear. But that too quickly ended.

A huge demon was approaching him from the left. The monster was at least eight feet tall. It was covered with a scaly skin that appeared to be rotting. Its head was enormous even for its body size. The demon didn't

have horns, rather the entire top of its head looked like a horn. A pointed nose sloped down into a wide set angry mouth. The teeth pointed down past its bottom lip.

The eyes were most terrifying. They were black with yellow rims. The eyes did not look at Jim. They seemed to be looking just past him. As the beast lumbered towards him its feet were kicking up the bones lying around him. The clacking sound of the bones knocking against other bones added to the fear. Jim could fill the evil emanating from the demon. Would his bones soon join those?

He knew they would not. He was here forever. This was not a logical thought. There was no reason to think this but he knew it more than he had ever known anything. Even death would bring him no relief. The terror and the horror would last for eternity. The demon walked right in front of him without even a sideways glance. Jim let out the smallest sigh of relief.

And then it grabbed him. It reached back and wrapped around Jim's entire body with a huge arm and drug him along its path. The top of his legs were being dragged through the bones and excrement below him. The heat exacerbated the pain of the quickly opening wounds. After twenty or thirty steps the beast slung him forward into a cell. The force of the throw was so sudden and violent that Jim was slammed against the back wall. The hot bricks of the wall scraped his body as he slid down.

He lied on the ground in pain and fear and moved his eyes to look at the demon. Beside him was a long wooden bench held in place with two thick black chains hanging off of the wall.

The demon was sitting on the bench. Its eyes focused ahead. It did not acknowledge Jim at all. The fear began to grow. He thought that this could not be possible. He was already so frightened that he could not imagine it getting worse. It did. The beast didn't care about him. He knew the thing didn't have any sympathy for him, or a way to process sympathy. It was a beast designed to torment and torture Jim Stahlhaber. He knew this perfectly. The demon could have been cutting wood, taking out trash or any

other mundane task. It just did. And what it did was beat Jim, its purpose, was to torture him.

After several long moments it stood up. Walked over to Jim and looked down at him.

"Stay here." It screamed. Then it bent down and picked Jim up by his left calf. It swirled him around and slammed him against the wall again. Its hands were huge claws and as it whipped him towards the wall he could feel the flesh being pulled from his lower leg.

He could feel and hear his skull cracking. Another sharp and intense shock of pain rose like lightening from the back of his legs to the top of his spine. The pain was too much. He could not endure it. And yet he knew he had no choice. He could not be knocked unconscious. This would not end.

The beast turned and walked out of the cell. Again with perfect purpose.

He laid still for several hours. He didn't dare move. When he thought he was finally safe he looked slowly down to his leg. The skin on his calf had healed. He reached gently up to touch his head. There was no fresh blood oozing and no wound to be felt.

He was no longer in any physical pain. But he was very uncomfortable. He had not moved from the position his body had taken after being slammed into the wall. He put his hands down to push himself up into a sitting position. His movements were deliberate and slow. At every movement he would stop and look around for the huge demon. When it did not return he would slide himself a little closer to the wall.

When he finally felt his back against the wall he relaxed. The smell was still there. The heat was still there. The discomfort still invaded every fiber of his being. The screams had gone. He could hear the bubbling cauldron pop and hiss sporadically. He tried to close his eyes but they were quickly forced open when he heard a faint laughing.

His arms went rigid as he braced himself on the floor. He didn't dare stand up. He pushed his back firmly against the wall. He could feel his heart beating. It was beating so hard he could see it pulsing in his chest. The laughter grew louder.

His eyes were focused intently at the opening of the small cell he was in. He could see three smaller demons approaching. They were laughing and talking in a language he could not understand and could not ever remember hearing before. They were walking towards the cell but did not pay attention to Jim or notice him.

He let himself slump ever so slightly. But the demons walked right in to the cell. They were still talking to each other and laughing. They did not look at him or acknowledge him in any way. Until they started kicking him. Then another was pulling his hair and slamming his head against the wall. This was pure malevolence with no purpose or meaning.

After a long time of torture they began to speak to him. But he could only understand every few words. Much of it was in the other language. They were saying terrible things about his mother, his father, his ex-wife and children. Jim could not process or articulate what they were saying clearly. But it frightened him more than the beating. When one would get close to his face he could smell its breath. It smelled like the feces and rotting flesh that was all around him.

When he was sure he could take no more, they continued to beat him. He could both feel and hear his bones breaking. And then they simply turned and walked away. They resumed their conversation and laughing. He was left alone again.

As soon as his body began to heal, only minutes after they had left, another group of demons came. There were only two this time. But the experience was the same. It was methodical, dispassionate torture. The demons wanted to kill him. But they could not. They would beat him and beat him. They would get angry that he would not die and beat him harder. Then they would give up and walk away.

The demons kept returning. The time between visits grew shorter. His body would heal only enough to allow the beating to continue.

Time was warped. He knew he had been hear for a very long time. But he could not measure it. There was no cycle to say this is one day or one hour. Time was measured only by the duration of the beating.

The huge demon returned. The one that had thrown him into the cell the very first time. This time Bob did not go rigid. There was no fight left in him. He felt nothing for the demon as it felt nothing for him. It was doing its job. His job was to take it. He knew this. He deserved this. He could not articulate any thought as to why he deserved this. He did not think about his previous life. He only knew that this was his life now. And that this was supposed to be.

The demon walked purposefully towards him. The massive arms swinging, the legs lumbering and kicking up bones. Jim waited. He waited for the beating and the pain. It was coming. This was fact and there was absolutely nothing that he could do to stop it.

As it entered his cell he scooted back instinctively, but then stopped himself. It would do no good. The beast was now towering above him. Something was different. This time it was looking directly in to Jim's eyes. It stared for just a second and then spoke.

"You did this."

Those three words were all that it said. It then turned and walked away. He dropped his head and looked down at his hands in his lap. Was something worse now coming?

He sat until he could no longer hear the footsteps of the demon. Then he slowly lifted his head and began to look around. The awful smell began to subside. The ground began to flatten and the bubbling stopped. He slowly rose to his feet. The walls of his cell began to melt into the ground around

him. A light fog that had wafted along the ground began to dissipate. And darkness began to settle around him.

Jim was alone now and the fear was new. He was alone forever. The beatings and the torture would not continue. They weren't coming back. This was a new dread. After the first demon had smashed his skull in to the wall and ripped the flesh from his leg it had ended. There had been a respite.

Now even that was gone. The hope for respite had left with the torture. Somehow this was even worse. The ground below him was no longer covered with bones, flesh or feces. It was hard packed earth and stone. His body had healed again. There was no sound. There was nothing to see.

He slumped slowly to the ground. He wanted to sleep. But despite what he had been through he was not tired. He looked around. His eyes were open but he could see nothing.

He sat on the ground his body a sloppy mess. His legs splayed out uncomfortably in front of him. His head slumped forward and his hands were back in his lap. This is where he would be forever. There was no one to help him and no way out. Forever. That was a certainty. The fear and dread were now resignation. He could conceive of no way out and he knew that this was right. He was supposed to be here. This was his home for all of eternity. This is where he belonged. Alone.

He thought about his life. But even that was difficult. He knew he had been married. Or thought he had. But he could not remember his wife's name. He thought that at one point many years ago that he had had children. But he could not remember their names or what they looked like.

He was alone in the universe. There was nothing else and there was no other person. The only tangible sensation or thought he could muster clearly was that he was thirsty. If he could just find a glass of water he could get his brain to work again.

But what would his brain work on? He focused his mind as hard as he could but only thirst would occupy him.

The despair he felt was made worse by the resignation. It was horrible to be alone. But it was worse to be alone forever and without any happy memories. Where had they gone? Something must have brought him to this place. He was certain he had not been here forever. There was something before this. But he could not remember what it was. He must have been born at some point. He knew that. But who were his parents? Was he a parent? Did he have a wife?

Before he came to be alone he knew that there were other people. But he did not know any of them. He could not remember them. And yet he knew, however faintly, that there were memories. He had done other things before he got here. We wondered if any of them were happy memories. Could he search his mind and find something, anything, to make him smile.

Then suddenly, a brief flash of remembrance. A vision flitted through his mind of a man he had met once or twice. Or was the man someone he had just heard of? His inability to concentrate was infuriating. There was no tangible memory to focus on. Just the thought of a man and something that man had said. But who was it?

He focused harder and more intently on that fleeting image. He was sure days were passing. He had been here for so long. And he continued to focus on the man. Then it happened. He saw the man more clearly. He saw himself sitting at a table eating lunch. The man sat across from him.

There was another man to his left, and another to his right. The man in the center was important. That was the man in the image but he could not see his face or hear his voice. He did not remember the man the way he should. It did not make him happy to remember him. It did not bring a smile to his face. It was something to do and something to focus on. The man, for some reason he could not understand, was important.

He tried feverishly in his mind too look at the man on the right. There was a clue there. And then it became clear. It was a man named Bob Fisher. He was a customer. No! A vendor. He bought things from this man. But Bob was not the man he wanted to focus on. Who was with him?

He focused again. Focused with all of his might. He tried to open his eyes as wide as he could to see the man in the middle.

"Tom!" That was his name. And Tom was talking. He was telling a story about some kind of big problem he had. His wife had been injured badly. That's what it was. Tom was talking about his wife falling off of a cliff while hiking. She had slipped. She had fallen over a hundred feet.

The conversation became clearer to Jim. It was as if he was sitting there. He remembered being amazed. The back pack she was wearing had snagged on a branch just as she was about to slam into rocks below her. It had flipped her body around and slowed her down just enough to allow her to land on her feet. She had broken her ankle and right leg.

But why was this important? Why was this all he could remember?

The conversation continued and Jim could hear himself talking.

"That is really lucky Tom. Your wife has to be about the luckiest person I've ever heard of."

Then he saw himself and his sarcastic smile. "You should tell your old lady to play the lottery because she is one lucky lady."

Tom's smile had left his face. He looked into Jim eyes. Deeper than any man ever had. At the time it had made Jim very uncomfortable. But now it did not. He just wanted to be able to remember what this man had said to him. He knew the man was speaking directly to him. He could see the change in Tom. There were only two people at the table. There were only two people in the restaurant and only two people in the entire world. Tom looked directly at him and said,

"It really wasn't luck. With Jesus Christ anything is possible. He can save you from falling off of a cliff and he can change your entire life in an instant."

He remembered it now. He remembered an awkwardness at the table. Bob and the man to the left of him had chuckled and tried to change the conversation quickly. Bob knew this man. Bob worked with him. They were talking to each other and trying to include Jim in the conversation. But his eyes did not leave the eyes of Tom Lawson. For a long time he just stared at him. It had been one of the few times in his life that he had been out of control. He was opened up to this man and Tom Lawson seemed to know it. Without saying a single word he had revealed so much to the man.

Why was he thinking about this now?

A new seed. Something else had been planted. Tom had mentioned a name. Another important name. Or was it a thing?

Jesus Christ. That's the name. He said nothing is impossible. His mind began to focus again. Jim had been to church. He had been to Christian churches. Not often. Probably not twenty times in his entire life. But he knew that name.

It hit him. Jesus Christ. Tom Lawson was trying to tell him something. He was trying to tell him that Jesus could save him! Or wait, Jesus could talk to God. Maybe that was it. He could be saved, that is what was important. He was not sure how it would work, he did not know how to pray or what thing he should do, but he knew he could be saved.

Jim knew this instinctively when Tom had said it just a couple of years ago. He knew it clearer than anything he had ever known. But he had walked away from it. He liked his life the way it was. He remembered that now. His life was a mess, but he had money and nice stuff. He could buy everything he needed. Even friends. But Lawson had messed him up for a few days because he knew the man was right. Jesus could save him. And

Jesus could save him from this. He had known it all along and chose to avoid the truth.

With every fiber of his body he knew that God could pull him out of this hell.

He cried out, "Jesus! Save me!"

OUT OF HELL

nd he did.

A hole opened up above him and a brilliant light flooded around Jim's body. The heat and the fear were completely gone. He felt a comfortable warmth. As if he were just two years old and his mother was hugging him.

And then a hand reached down to him. The hand pulled him up through the light. He felt a warmth and love wash over him. He started to smile.

The hand dropped him gently on his feet. Now everything around him was light. A lone man stood in front of him. Jim really was home. This was where he wanted to be. This is where he belonged. He was filled with complete joy. There was no pain, no worry and no sorrow. There was only a peace and love in him and around him.

The man was looking at Jim but he did not speak. Jim did not try to speak either. He just wanted to feel this love. He noticed flashes in his peripheral vision. He turned to look as images of his life played out in small screens all around him.

Every image was something that he had done wrong. But what made it so much worse is that every single instance that was shown he remembered clearly. He remembered that at the time he knew was doing the wrong thing, he knew it was wrong. And he did it anyway.

He saw his ex-wife Olivia and his children. They were connected. He could see it. He could see lines, or strings connecting them. He could see

his father yelling at him in high school. He could see his mother. A nice woman who lived her life. Jim could see that she loved him but could not, or would not show it.

He saw a very small child. Just a baby. Jim knew that the baby was his little sister. He knew that she had died shortly after birth. But neither his mother nor father ever spoke of her.

He saw people he worked with. He saw women he had dated. He saw every interaction that had been wrong. He was taking advantage of people. He was lying to his wife and children. He was lying to so many people. He saw himself in his office late at night changing accounting records and personnel records. All things he was doing to make more money for himself.

There were brief glimpses of happiness. Small times in his life that were important chances. When his children were born was a chance. He knew he had to change his life. For a few days he would ponder making changes. But he would not. When he saw that he was not going to change he could see the connections causing pain. There were so many of these opportunities. Never once did he do the right thing.

His mind was working clearly now. He saw what he had done wrong and he felt ashamed. But just as quickly he started to remember the bad things that had happened to him. His grandmother that he loved so much and been so important to him had died. His father had been much the same as Jim had. He had been distant. His mother was the same. Although he was sure the loss of his baby sister had contributed, it had not been his fault.

A girl that he had loved had left him. It was when Jim was first in college. He had fallen hard for the girl but he had gotten drunk one night and slept with a girl he did not know. His girlfriend had found out about it and left him. He knew what he had done was wrong, but she had never given him a second chance. So many times in his life he could remember not being able to connect with another single human being. When he did

something wrong to someone they left him. So he had done the same. As he got older he never even gave anyone the chance to wrong him.

He turned away from the images and looked at the man before him. The man's eyes were looking so deeply into Jim that he could feel the man knew everything about him. He felt loved by the man. He felt a love all around him and deep inside him. After all that he had done this person still loved him. He knew this man was either God or Jesus. He wished he would speak. After what seemed like a very long moment he did speak.

"Why are you here?"

"I want to stay here with you." Was all that Jim could muster. It was the only thought he had.

"You cannot. You are not ready." The man answered.

Jim was nothing if not persistent. He was going to stay here. He had too.

"No one loves me back there. I've made a mess of everything. I have no friends and my family wants nothing to do with me. I don't like the work I do and there is nothing for me and no one who cares for me."

"You're right. Now go fix it."

Jim was adamant. He wanted to stay. He wanted to spend eternity feeling this love and warmth. He had to stay. "I don't even know where to start! I don't know what to do back there. You love me and I want to stay here."

"Bob Fisher will help you. You are not ready. Go and make the best of it."

"But who is Bob Fisher? And what...."

Before he could get the sentence out he was falling. He turned his head to see his body still lying on the floor in his office. He saw medical workers running in to help.

"How can I still be here? I've been gone for months. Years maybe." Was his last thought.

And then he was back in his body.

JIM IS ALIVE

Someone was talking. Jim struggled to open his eyes. His entire body was sore and he just wanted to sleep. But someone kept calling his name.

He finally managed to peak out of one eye. A doctor was bending over his bed and just inches from Jim's face.

"Hey Jim, I need you to talk to me for just a second okay?"

He nodded slightly.

"How is the pain?"

Jim smiled. "I'm sore all over. But it's really much better. I don't feel like an elephant is standing on my chest anymore."

The doctor laughed politely. "That's great Jim."

"Did I have a heart attack?"

"Yes. But you're going to be feeling much better. You had one artery that was almost completely blocked. It may have been lifestyle related but I suspect it was partially just genetics. We put a stent in to open it up and now everything is looking really great. You should be out of here in just a few days."

"Out of where?" Jim asked.

"You're in the CCU, Cardiac Care Unit at St. Agnes hospital. The ambulance brought you in late yesterday. It's Saturday morning about....." The doctor looked at his watch. "Looks like it's about 10:30 in the morning.

My name is Doctor Singh and I installed your stent. Are you call caught up now?"

Jim didn't like doctors. So many of them were so damned condescending.

"Yeah thanks Doc, we're all good. Sorry to bother you but I've got a fairly large business to run and need to know when I can get back at it."

"I understand completely Mr. Stahlhaber. We'll get you back on your feet as soon as humanly possible."

Jim knew the doctor had felt chastised. He noticed the switch from the friendly "Jim" to the more respectful "Mr. Stahlhaber."

He closed his eyes satisfied that he had handled the doctor in just the right way. As he started to drift off to sleep his eyes opened suddenly and he was wide awake. He started to sit up in his bed but the pain was too much. He settled his head back to his pillow. He very much wanted to call out to the doctor and apologize. For a second he wondered why. Jim Stahlhaber was not a man that ever needed to apologize. And then the vision faintly crept in to his mind. He shuddered. It was just a dream. Wasn't it?

"Nurse!" He yelled.

A young male nurse was quickly beside him. "Yes Mr. Stahlhaber, can I get you something."

"I'm just in a lot of pain. Can I get more pain medicine now? Or is it too soon? Even just something to help me sleep would probably be fine. I don't want to bug you and whatever you think is best. I'm just really uncomfortable."

He hoped the young man didn't see through him. He was in pain. But it was bearable. He just didn't want to think about what had happened when he had the heart attack. He didn't have the strength to think about it right

now. He was certain it had just been a bad dream. But he really didn't want to think about Hell.

"Yes Mr. Stahlhaber. We'll get you fixed right up and it's no trouble it all. That's why I'm here."

The nurse smiled, reached over Jim's body and turned a dial on one of the machines above his head. And just like that he could feel the medicine numbing his mind and body. He quickly fell back in to a deep, drug induced, sleep.

Early in the evening the sound of voices woke him up. Olivia and his two kids were standing by his bed. "Hey Dad, how are you feeling?" His son spoke first. He smiled and looked at all three of them.

"I'm doing much better now. Olivia. Thank you so much for coming."

She smiled and patted his arm softly. He looked at his young daughter Jessica. She was pretty like her mother. He felt tears welling up in his eyes and fought to keep them at bay. Olivia moved back slightly allowing Jessica in closer. He lifted his right arm to give her a hug.

"I'm so happy you're okay Daddy." She said through tears.

It was the sweetest thing Jim had heard in many years. He tried to reach his son Kyle's hand with his left hand but the boy had taken a step back.

"Is there anything you need Jim?" Olivia asked.

"I'm just so happy all of you are here Olivia." He answered. He saw the confusion is Olivia's face. This was not the answer she expected.

He looked at his son. "Hey Kyle. Mom said you got National Honors Society. Way to go! I'm so proud of you. But I've always been proud of both you kids. You sure deserve a better father than you got stuck with, but maybe that's why you ended up with such a great mom."

He laughed at his own little joke. Kyle just nodded politely. "Thanks Dad." But he felt Jessica squeeze him a little tighter.

It was uncomfortable for everyone. Jessica was trying and he felt a familiar connection with Olivia. Kyle was just slightly less distant than normal. But Jim could feel it, they were all uncomfortable. He knew, and they all knew his little joke had more than a grain of truth to it. They tried to make small talk for a few minutes. Nothing of substance. Kyle had finally had enough. "Hey Mom we really need to get going. I have that thing tonight."

Jim caught the stern glance from Olivia towards his son. He wanted to diffuse the situation and the truth was he was also growing very uncomfortable.

"It's okay Hon." He said to Olivia. He hadn't called her Hon in probably five years. And certainly not since the divorce almost six months ago. "I'm sure he's got stuff to do."

Olivia was again visibly taken back. She patted Jim's arm again and smiled genuinely at him.
"Are you sure there isn't anything you need?" She asked.

He hesitated a moment. He knew what he wanted but he was afraid. After a long pause he finally responded. "I'm supposed to be getting out of here on Wednesday. But is there any chance you could stop by tomorrow or Monday? It just gets really boring around here."

"I'll stop by Monday after work. Would that be good?" She asked.

"That would be perfect. And hey, I know you kids have stuff to do. I'll stop by and see you when I get out of here."

By Sunday afternoon Jim could not believe how much better he felt. He was sore to be sure but he could feel that he was getting better by the hour. He thought about asking the doctor if he could get out a day early. He needed to beat the odds. He needed to get back to work and show everyone

he was still in charge and still in great shape. The hospital had moved him out of the CCU and to a private room. He had made a few phone calls to his people at work. No one had come to visit him from the office, but he didn't care. There were flowers and cards from vendors. Nothing from anyone else, but that was to be expected.

He noticed that Bob Fisher hadn't sent him any flowers or a get well card. The thought led his mind in a way he didn't want to go. So he pushed it back down. He had to get that crazy dream out of his mind. He had to get back to his life. He would make a few changes. He knew some of it had been his subconscious telling him to be a better father. And he would do that. Jessica and Kyle deserved a better father than he had had and he would deliver.

He spent most of the day Monday talking on the phone. Things at the office were going just fine, but he needed to feel important. He talked to the production manager, sales director and VP and even found an excuse to talk to the maintenance manager. He even managed to flirt with Lexi a few times while calling in. By the time Olivia finally showed up he was starting to get tired. But he was happy with how the day had progressed.

When she walked into his room he found himself momentarily speechless. Olivia truly was a beautiful woman. He had married her because she was stunningly beautiful. She was nearly five feet ten inches tall. She had dark brown hair that was long and wrapped around the edges of her face. A perfect nose, perfect chin, perfect high cheek bones and the most beautiful eyes he had ever seen.

If he was going to have a wife, this was what he wanted her to look like. After dating for a few months he realized that she was also a genuinely nice person. She rarely argued. She was quiet but intelligent. For years she had been the perfect bride for Jim. She didn't ask too many questions.

She loved to spend money on herself and then later on the kids and he didn't mind giving it to her. They had slowly grown apart. But when he

needed her she was there. He would take her to important dinners with potential customers. She was so cultured and gorgeous that he knew other men couldn't resist her.

At a fancy formal dinner for a politician or some charity that he was attending she would be the perfect accessory. Those charity dinners were a great place to make new contacts and everyone wanted to talk to Olivia.

And then she changed. He remembered the day. It was a Saturday afternoon just a couple of years ago. He had just walked in the door after a morning of golf. She was sitting in the white chair in the family room crying. The kids weren't home. She was all alone just sitting in that chair crying. He had rushed to her side. His first thought was that her mother or father had died. But when he tried to talk to her, when he tried to ask her what had happened she just looked right through him.

When she composed herself she told him there was something missing in her life. But now he recalled that's not exactly what she said. She said our lives.

"Jim, we aren't living right. We are missing something in our lives."

H had laughed at her. This had not made her mad, it had confused her. So he told her she was just starting to get closed to middle age and she had been stuck in the house with the kids for too long. He tried to talk her into taking a vacation by herself or with a friend. He tried to get her to buy a new car. Nothing worked. They had talked for hours and made no progress. When the kids finally came home she simply wiped her eyes and ended the conversation.

Over the next few months she had gotten into Buddhism, crystals, and all kinds of other spiritual things. Nothing seemed to work. She had withdrawn from him. She would still go to his dinners and meetings if he asked. She wasn't the same.

Shortly before the divorce she had started going to some church in town. Just some non-denominational Christian church. He had tried to go with her once. It just wasn't his thing. The preacher, or pastor or priest, whatever the guy was who ran the church, seemed like a nice guy. He talked about living a happy life. He read a little from the bible. And he wasn't one of those guys that was fire and brim stone and talking about going to Hell.

And then Jim snapped himself out of the memory. Hell. He didn't want to think about Hell.

"Olivia, thank you so much for coming. Where are the kids?"

He knew she would see through him as soon as he said it. He had specifically asked her not to bring the kids on Saturday. He saw the change in her face.

"Jim, you told me not to bring them. Do you want me to leave now?"

He was trapped. The answer was yes. He wanted her gone. If she was here he would think about that church. He would think about Hell. And he didn't want to do that. He wanted that awful dream out of his mind. But he had to save face.

"Oh did I?" His mind was working fast. This is what he was good at. He could come up with a lie to get him out of a jam quicker than any man alive.

"I guess I was foggy from the pain meds. Ha! Why wouldn't I want the kids to come? Well Olivia, I'm glad you came. You look very nice."

She managed only a slight smile in return. He knew the look. She was frustrated with him. She knew he was lying to her. What made it worse was he knew she knew. He had been here hundreds of times. Jim was a liar and Olivia knew it. But even when he lied to her it was an innocent lie. For years she had played the game.

But this time she didn't. Her eyes never left his. She did not surrender this time and he didn't like it. She held his gaze for several seconds.

"Jim I still love you and suppose I always will. There is something good inside you somewhere. But if having a heart attack and almost dying doesn't change you, I don't think anything ever will. If you aren't going to fix your life now, I guess it really is over."

"What the hell Olivia? I just had a heart attack. Sorry if I'm not on my "A" game. And it wasn't some huge heart attack. The doc said I didn't even sustain any permanent damage. It was one blocked artery that was just a genetic defect and it's all fixed. I'm still a little sore from the surgery. But I didn't almost die Olivia. You're making too much of this."

He wished she would leave. But she just kept starting at him.

"The doctor said your heart stopped Jim."

He just waved his hand in a dismissive gesture. "That's what a heart attack is Olivia. It's not a big deal." He didn't know if that was true or not. But he knew he had to get her out of his presence.

"Look, I really appreciate you stopping by, but I am still recovering from the surgery and I'm really tired."

She stared at him again for a few seconds. He could not read her face. He dared not say another word. He was afraid of what he would say and just as afraid of what she might say. "Okay Jim, I'll leave."

Alone again with his thoughts he made a decision. He was going to confront this thing. This horrible dream. He had a life of plenty. Plenty of money. Plenty of power and plenty of stability. He could quit work right now and sell the company to Hauser Hamilton Aerospace and be set for life.

He bolted up in his bed. The pain was not noticeable. The lie was. It had been real and he knew it. Some may have followed Jesus, God or a religion on blind faith, but he could not. That crutch had been kicked away

from him. He did not need faith, because he had seen the truth. He knew better. They sky was blue. The grass was green. Hell was real and he had seen God and Heaven.

It wasn't a dream. He was there. The fear, the anguish and the loneliness came flooding back to him. And then the feeling of love and warmth when God had pulled him out of hell came back to him.

Bob, Jim and Tom

I t was Wednesday afternoon. Bob glanced at the clock on his phone. It was 3:00 PM.

In just three hours his life would start over. He was going to meet Tom for dinner and figure out a way to come work with him. He had no idea how to make this happen. The good news was that Donna was fully on board.

They had called the realtor and the house was up for sale. He would have to stay on his job until they sold the house and bought a new one. He had spent all night Tuesday on a budget. Donna wanted to get a job as well. With both of them working they figured that Bob could quit his job in four or five months. They should be able to save five thousand dollars by then. That would give them a little breathing room. They could raise more money by having a garage sale. The stainless steel electric trash container would have to go. As would a bunch of other things they had bought and didn't need.

He had been honest with Donna. He told her that this could bankrupt them. But it wouldn't stop his mission. If Tom would have him and they could just get started, this is what he wanted to do. This is what he had to do.

He laughed to himself. This is what he had always wanted. A big job a big title and a fat paycheck. And now he was going to walk away from it all. If he could make the budget work he would be leaving his old dreams behind in just about four months. Maybe six at the longest. But that was the limit.

He had made a commitment to himself. He would leave this job and began his new life as an associate pastor in six months. He was not entirely sure how he was going to do this. But he knew it was going to happen. Somehow, some way, this would all work out.

His phone buzzed. It was Betty. The receptionist.

"Mr. Fisher there is a Jim Stahlhaber here to see you. Should I send him up?"

"Who?" Bob asked. Knowing she couldn't have said Jim Stahlhaber.

"It's a Mr. Jim Stahlhaber. He said he is a friend of yours and that you sometimes work together."

"Sure Betty, send him up."

"What could this be about?" Bob wondered. He knew Stahlhaber had had a heart attack a few weeks back. But he hadn't talked to him since or heard anything at all about his condition. He unconsciously braced himself for whatever catastrophe had brought the man all the way from California. Just a few moments later he heard a soft knock on his door.

"Come in." He said as he stood from his desk and walked to welcome him.

Bob was instantly taken aback. He had never seen Stahlhaber without a tailored suit, shiny shoes, the latest style tie and a matching handkerchief in his breast pocket. Today he was wearing tan cargo pants, a long sleeve thermal shirt and he had sneakers on. His usually perfectly combed and slightly oiled hair was a bit longer now and while not sloppy at all, just looked quite natural on him.

"Well... Hello Jim, to what do I owe the pleasure of your visit?" The minute the words came out of his mouth Bob felt stupid. Why had he always been able to make him feel like a stupid kid?

But too his surprise Stahlhaber burst out laughing. He laughed so loud that several people outside Bob's office peaked in.

He then walked up to Bob and shook his hand warmly. The smile never left his face. "I never thought I'd hear you say, or honestly deserve to hear you say that my visit was a pleasure to you."

Bob was becoming more confused by the second. But Stahlhaber's smile and attitude were infectious. He could not help but smile himself.

"Nonsense Jim! It is good to see you. I know we've never actually been friends, just business associates, but I heard about your heart attack and I'm so glad that you are okay." Bob motioned for Jim to take a seat at one of the chairs in front of his desk, then set himself down behind it.

"So what brings you out here? No problems with that last order I hope." Bob said.

"I really wouldn't know Bob. I sold the company to Hauser and Hamilton two weeks ago. And it is wonderful to see you as well. I heard about your car accident. From the looks of those crutches it seems like you are at least on the mend.

And now that you know I don't own the business, or even have a job anymore you're probably really wondering why I'm bothering you. Well, to tell you the truth, I just need a simple favor that I hope you'll grant me.

A few years ago you brought a man out with you to one of our meetings. It was one of those lunch meetings where I acted like a complete jerk and everyone goes along with it because I was paying the bills. The man you brought with you was named Tom Lawson. I'd like to get in touch with him if you could arrange that. I understand that he is no longer employed here."

"Uhh, sure Jim. I guess I could do that. But may I ask why?"

"Because God told me to" Stahlhaber answered just as a simple matter of fact.

Bob's entire body went rigid and he could feel the blood draining from his face. This caused Stahlhaber to laugh again.

"Oh I know that look! Three weeks ago that look and your tension would have been on my face and in my body. But it's getting easier by the minute. You see Bob, when I had my heart attack I had one of those near death experiences. Ever heard of that?" Jim asked.

Bob just nodded in disbelief.

"Well, anyway" Jim continued, "When I had mine I didn't go to Heaven like most people do. I had been a bad person my whole life so I went to Hell. But God, or maybe Jesus, I'm not too sure, pulled me out of there. Oh, I wanted to stay but he made me come back here.

When I was in Hell I remembered something Tom Lawson had told me. He said with Jesus anything is possible. And I guess I cried out to Jesus or something because just then I was pulled out of Hell by a man or an angel. I was trying to talk him into letting me stay dead and in Heaven, but he wouldn't let me. When I told him I didn't know how to live a good life or even how to start he told me, 'Bob Fisher will help you' so here I am."

I figured God said that because you know Tom Lawson and you were the one who introduced me to him. So I think you're supposed to help me find Tom Lawson and that's how you can help me.

And Bob all I can tell you is the way you are cringing right now is the same way I used to cringe when people talked about Jesus, and God and religion and all that. And I don't know anything else in the world other than God wants you to help me. He wants you to help me find Tom Lawson.

"I...." Was the only word Bob could speak.

He noticed a look of concern on Jim's face.

"Bob I'm sorry. I didn't mean to lay so much on you like that. I'm just really learning about all of this and I suppose I got a little too

comfortable and came on to strong. I know religion and God are all a bit much for most people today. I'm sorry if I made you uncomfortable."

Finally Bob let out the air that had been building in his lungs and he smiled and chuckled.

"No. It's not that. It's not that at all.

"Jim, when I had my car accident, I too died. I went to Heaven. I met an Angel named Samuel. He told me I was living my life wrong. He told me many of us were living our lives wrong and that I was supposed to come back and tell people that they need to connect to their spiritual side.

And over the last few weeks I've gotten to know Tom Lawson pretty well. In fact, he and I are going to have dinner tonight at six. I am going to quit this job as soon as I can afford it and go work with Tom. The reason he left is he is going to start his own church. And I want to go with him. I am going to help him and I am going to be a preacher someday I guess. I'm in the same boat as you. I don't know much about any of this. I just know what happened to me was real. And if there was any lingering doubt, well, now that you are here it is completely gone. So I guess we are both going to have dinner with Tom Lawson tonight."

When he had finished it was Jim's turn to be shocked.

* * *

At dinner that night Tom Lawson was stunned. He knew what had happened to Bob but Jim's story had thrown him like nothing ever had in his life. He knew that this was going to be bigger than he had ever imagined. He mission in life to start a small church had been altered. All three men were silent after Jim finished his story of Hell.

"So what is our mission and how do we get started?" Tom asked.

. "Well, I think you know a lot more about The Bible and religion than either Jim or I. So maybe you should lead this." Bob said.

"That's not what this is about anymore. You and Jim have had an experience that is truly out of this world. I saw myself as the pastor of a small church. My thought was to help a congregation. A few hundred people at most. I thought I would learn with them. But now? I think this is much bigger. You two must be at the forefront. It has to be your message. It has to be your mission. I will help. I want to help. But I want to hear what you two believe we should do."

Jim spoke first and was quick to respond. "I'm just here to learn. I know I have to change my life, and I've already started. God told me to see Bob Fisher. So I did. But I thought I was only supposed to see him to get to you Tom. Like I said before, I think it was you that got me out of Hell. What if you hadn't said those words to me? Where would I be now? So that's it for me. I'm here to learn. I'll work with you and do what I can. But for me this journey is one day at a time. To be honest, I feel like it's one hour at a time."

Tom nodded at Jim and then looked to Bob. "What do you think Bob?"

"I'm the same. I know what Samuel told me. But I don't know how church works. I don't know how to set one up or anything else about running a church. All that I can do is stand up there on a podium and talk about what I saw and what the angel told me.

But I also don't have any money yet. I figured over the next four or five months I could save enough to join your church as an assistant. Donna is going to work and I can also work part time. But this is what I want to focus on. I guess I didn't realize that this would take money!"

Tom laughed. "I always knew it would. It will either work or it won't. If you get your house sold I still think we are on track to start in six months at the latest. I've been looking at places we can rent on the cheap and

trying to figure out the cost to turn an old drug store into a church. But I guess that gives us time to get our plan together.

Are you still working Jim?"

"No. But I think I know what my first purpose is in this mission." He answered.

Stahlhaber reached behind his back and pulled a check book out. "I sold my company Tom. I got thirty million dollars in cash. The taxes were a little under six million. I gave my ex-wife four million. And I hope someday she will be my wife again. But if not, she will be able to take care of herself and my kids forever. Then I gave five million dollars away to different churches and five million dollars to my sister and brother. That leaves me with about ten million dollars. "

Tom and Bob's eyes both grew wide. Jim put his check book on the dinner table and began writing. "Do you have a name for this church yet Tom?" He asked.

A sheepish smile came over Tom's face. "I'm not much of a marketing guy. The only thing I could come up with is 'The church of hope, love and life." He answered.

"Catchy." Bob added smiling.

Jim tore a check from the book and handed it to Tom. "Now I have no money at all. And though I cannot bring anything much to the table other than this money, I hope you'll give me a job so I can feed myself and rent a place to live. I really only need about twenty thousand per year and I won't take more than that. But now you have ten million dollars. So let's get started."

Bob was shaking his head in disbelief. He tried to protest. He insisted that it was way too much money. But Jim just put his hand up and said; "It is the easiest thing I have ever done."

Tom was unchanged. Bob looked at him and waited for him to say something. But Tom just stared back at him silently. After a long pause he spoke;

"After what has happened to you two to bring us together, I think this is just another part of the miracle. I have no words. I do not know how or why this happened. But I feel a great responsibility."

"My trip to Hell and Bob's trip to Heaven were miracles perhaps Tom. But not this money. I never earned a penny of it. From the time I inherited the business from my father it got worse and less profitable every single day. I was lucky to keep it running as long as I did. A woman who gives twenty dollars at church and is left with eighty dollars for groceries does way more than I did."

"You know Jim, it pretty much says that exact same thing in The Bible." Tom said.

"It does?" Jim asked, a smile and look of surprise on his face.

"Yes. But we still appreciate it. And I still think it's a miracle."

For several minutes there was an awkward silence. Bob and Tom glanced at each other uncomfortably. What do you say when someone hands you millions of dollars? And it is all the money they have. It was Jim who finally broke the silence.

"Ever since Bob told me about his experience I've been wondering something. Why did this happen?"

"I've been wondering the same thing." Bob responded.

"Samuel the angel told me it was because we had become separated from our spiritual selves. That we were living one life, the physical. But why me? Why us? Why now?"

THE MISSION AND THE MESSAGE

I t's because it's all changed.

Tom answered them both.

"For years I've been thinking about it. Life has changed so much and so quickly for so many people. Man has walked this earth for tens of thousands of years. And very quickly, just about 100 years ago it really started to change.

Did you know that just a few hundred years ago most people never travelled more than thirty or forty miles from where they were born? They lived small physical lives. But more of them had a spiritual side.

The Native American Indians had "The Great Spirit in the Sky!" They knew that there feet were planted on this earth, but that there was something else they were connected too. They didn't feel so alone. I think people may have been happier back then. When something terrible happened they knew it was only happening to a part of them. The physical part. Bad things could only hurt so much. But there is also a spiritual part."

Haven't you really felt a spiritual pull always? Haven't you thought you were connected to something bigger?"

"I always have." Bob answered first. "There were times in my life where I would think about it more than others. I would go to church for a few weeks. I would read the bible occasionally. Maybe even listen to one of those television preachers, but I never would stick with it. I knew something was pulling me, or trying to talk to me. I just didn't listen and I guess it never really grew with me."

"I always knew." Jim said. "I fought it my entire life. There were times when I was sure that I had more faith in God than the pope himself. It scared me. I knew what I was. I knew what I was doing and I knew it was wrong. I used money to hide from life. And this isn't some grand realization. I knew it all along. I wasn't just running from God, I was running and hiding from anything good.

You both think it was some great sacrifice to write you that check. It wasn't. It was the easiest thing I've ever done. I know I had an empty life. And living like that is a huge burden.

I thought I had friends. I thought I had a family and I tried to convince myself that I was happy. But I was miserable and hateful. I never really knew any of my friends. I don't really even know my own kids. I know my ex-wife is a very good person. I know where she was born, her birthday and the names of her relatives. I know where she went to high school and college.

But I don't know anything about her. I just know she didn't deserve me. I talked to people all day every day. Either in person, on the phone or with email I was always with and around other people. But I was always lonely. I've been on this earth for more than forty years and if you looked back on my life you would find not one single thing that was significant. But I know that is going to change."

"It's funny what you said about being around people all the time." Tom said.

"Today our kids can have friends all over the world. They talk to them on their phones and have messages back and forth on the internet in real time. But they don't really connect do they?"

"At least they have someone to talk to, lots of people as you said right?" Bob interjected.

"That's true, but they don't have those deep connections. Look around our office Bob.

Jim, you had money and I'm sure you know dozens of people who have money. Are they happy?"

Jim shook his head slowly from side to side as if a profound realization had struck him.

"You know something? I always thought it was just me. But not one of my inner circle ever seemed happy either."

"I just don't think God created us to live like this."

Tom continued. "I used to think it was because we had become so material. Everyone just wants to buy more and more stuff. But that's not it. It's something bigger. People are buying stuff because they are trying to fill a hole. They are bored. They are empty and they are confused. "

Bob was hanging on Tom's every word. He remembered what Samuel had told him.

"Life is serious business. I don't want to sound old fashioned but one of the things that Samuel taught me was that sometimes when we pray we should be on our knees. He said we do that because prayer is so important. There are those who say, 'We live on this earth and that is how we should live our lives. We should focus on the physical.' I know others that say, 'We are here only for a short time, we should focus our lives on Heaven and the after-life.' But I think what Samuel was telling me is that both are true."

"Yes, it is a very short time but I can tell you this, when you are in Hell it's a very long time. I could not have been there for more than two or three minutes. They told me my heart had only stopped for a minute or two. Yet it felt like I was there for months or even years."

"So what do we do?" Tom asked.

"This may be one place I can help." Jim answered. "I know what our first step is. It's to live our lives the best we can. If we live with no other purpose than to love each other and love everyone we come across, well that alone will be a big help."

"That's a good summary of what Samuel said." Bob added. "We are all connected. We should be living our lives on earth to learn so that we can live in Heaven."

"Sorry to asked stupid questions." Jim said. "Remember, I'm new to all of this. But why wouldn't God have just made us in Heaven?"

"Because Heaven is forever." Tom answered. "If we are here only for a little while what do we do with our time? There are certain things we have to do. We have to work to eat, have shelter and clothing. We have to work to provide for our families. And maybe while we're doing that we work a little harder.

Maybe that's one of the things we learn. That if we work we can provide for those who can't. We can help each other. But writing checks isn't enough. We have to connect. We have to learn to not just tolerate each other, but to get along and love each other.

Look at our world today. We all judge each other. We judge each other based on political beliefs, religious beliefs, even the clothes we wear and the area we live in."

"That's a good point Tom." Jim said. The biggest impact on my life so far has been that I don't judge people anymore. It's made me happier

already. I used to judge everyone. Every single person I could find fault with. Like I said, I didn't even know those people.

I think I'm starting to see what you were talking about Tom. In the past people would not have judged each other based on the clothes they wore. At least not as much as we do now. But today, heck just watch television. Everything you see and hear is about how to make your life materially better than someone else.

I bought it hook line and sinker. I just went along with whatever the TV told me to do. And it was so meaningless. It gave me a license. A license to look down on you if you didn't drive a certain kind of car. Or didn't live in a certain kind of house."

"It doesn't work, does it?" Bob said.

"Not one little bit." They both laughed at Jim's answer and Bob continued.

"I did the same thing. Probably on a smaller scale but I did it.

This is what's wrong in the world. We are living fake lives like zombies. We go through motions. We live a completely physical life. We do it because we are afraid. Afraid of what the neighbors might think. Afraid that our families might not think we're successful enough. Afraid that we might not measure up to an actor on a television show or in a commercial.

Does it help? Does any of it make us one bit happier? It only makes the guy who sold you the new car or computer happy. It only makes the billionaires happy who own the big companies. The rest of us just continue to be zombies."

"You're wrong Bob."

Jim said. "I've met billionaires that own the big companies. The tech millionaires that sell and develop new software and live in mansions in California, they aren't happy either. They're just bigger zombies."

Bob nodded.

"I guess that just makes sense. What happened to us? What happened to human beings? Why do we keep living our lives like this? We aren't happy. We aren't even doing great things. We are living for the moment in tiny little bubbles, buying stupid little trinkets. And some of us are all alone."

"It's because we aren't thinking." Tom said.

"We've rented out our minds. Not to the highest bidder, but to the lowest. We've given up on thinking for ourselves. We listen to whoever offers the easiest path to the most stuff. If there is more of something, we figure it must be better.

I know that God put you two with me so that we could start to help people reconnect with the side of us that is lost. I think I may even know what to say. Especially with both of you here now. I know that there are consequences if we don't live right and rewards if we do. But the one thing I've always struggled with is why? Why are people going to listen to us? Why are they going to take time to come and hear what we have to say?

This is the nut I cannot crack. People have tried this for centuries. It used to work. But now people won't even go to church. How do we get them to want this?

"That's the easy part Tom." Jim said.

If they want to be happy here, and they want to go to Heaven, they have to change their lives. It's like Bob said, life is important.

But that doesn't mean it has to be suffering all the time. That doesn't mean it is to be meaningless here. Quite the opposite. It is meaningful and it can be filled with joy. Then, when the bad things happen, we'll be able to work through them. We'll understand that this earth isn't perfect, but what we're working towards is."

"I like that." Bob said.

"So do I." Tom replied. He took out a pen and a pad of paper and started writing.

"So this is our mission and the message."

1. You need to live your entire life. The spiritual and the physical. You are on earth, but your soul is connected to God. You should have ambition not just to make money, but to live a good life.

2. You are connected to each other. The billionaire, the preacher, the hobo and the restaurant manager are all connected. You are all important to each other. If you can't get along with someone because of the color of their skin or the kind of clothes they wear, how will you ever get in to Heaven?

3. You need to think about your life. This is work and needs to be respected. You need to use the brain God gave you to consider all things. If hate and fear are in your life, you need to first think about why. Then you will be able to understand that those things are hurting you.

4. Love connects us. Love makes everything possible.

> "I'd like to add one to that list." Bob said. When I was in Heaven I noticed something that was hard to describe.

5. Both I and We are important. We are all connected and we are important. We can help each other to make a better world. But you are important and I am important as individuals. I must be an individual. I must make myself better and happier. We are, and I am.

"I think that's pretty good." Tom said. "Jim, do you want to add anything?"

Jim sat still for a long time. He was clearly trying to put something in to words. He finally spoke.

"I know what people want. I know these five things will help them get there. But I think I know what everyone wants."

Bob and Tom leaned in slightly to make sure they could hear him.

"I want peace in my soul. To get that, I have to accept that God is real and that God is connected to me. I can get that peace when I pull my soul into my physical life. Then I will know that I am living my life in the right way and I will have peace.

ABOUT THE DATA AND RESEARCH

There is something to this.

The most compelling part of near death experiences are the out of body experiences that are verified by a third person. This is something the skeptics and the scientists are going to have to reckon with to have integrity in their research. There are simply too many of these occurrences to be statistically insignificant.

Many are verified by disinterested third parties. Often they report events going on outside of the room or even the building that they are in at the time of the experience. One man was in his house and saw the ambulance driver walking around the outside of the house looking for the door.

Another person tells of a specific patient who had died in another room. Still others talk of seeing friends or family members in other parts of the hospital. It is patently ridiculous to assume that all of these people are somehow colluding to create a fascinating story. There are currently scientific tests going on around the world right now to verify this.

Numbers are being placed above the lights and equipment in emergency rooms in some hospitals. If the person who has the near death experience relates the number we will have proof. But even here we run into a problem.

For years people who have these experiences say that the objects around their bodies are transparent. They can see through ceilings, walls and we must assume medical equipment. The other problem with this approach is it could take a very long time to work. I would imagine if you

were looking down on your body from the ceiling of a hospital room as you are dying the last thing you would take note of would be a number written on a piece of paper on top of some equipment.

I really cannot conceive of how this is more trustworthy than the words of all of these witnesses who validate the stories. Won't the die-hard skeptics claim that there was some collusion between the dying person and someone else in the room who told them the number?

To come up with the story of Bob Fisher's fictional story I read and analyzed thousands of stories by people who had a near death experience. As a data analyst by trade I put all of the data into a SQL database, created meta-data trying to find consistent patterns and then delve in to the consistencies.

One of the things that I kept noticing was that some people would see a tree with brilliantly colored leaves. So I created a section of data called tree. This column would simply have Y or N as the response. So I analyze the data and anywhere the word "tree" is in the description I put a "Y" in the column. Then I can sort by all of the experiences (about 22%) where there is mention of a tree.

But as I would go through the data and start to read those stories I had to remove some of the stories. The only way to do this is to add another column about trees. In this column I had to put "relevant?" as a column. This is because a surprising number of people have near death experiences after falling out of a tree! Of course others may have had a heart attack or some other injury and they were laying under a tree. So the word "tree" is in the text, but it is not relevant.

The first thing you begin to understand is that most of the people who have these experiences aren't writers and don't go into much detail. This is especially true for people who have an NDE as children and recount the experience many years later. For some of these all that we can tell is that they had a very profound experience that has made them unafraid of dying.

Within these one or two paragraph narratives there is still an incredible consistency. They talk about feeling an incredible love and peace. They talk about seeing a brilliant light and they will tell you that there sense of time was not the same as it is on earth.

On the other end of the spectrum you will find stories that go in to great detail. It is very tempting to give higher priority to these stories but I resisted that urge. The reason is that it appears to me that some of these

stories, while not embellished, tend to fit too closely with cultural or religious influences.

Early in my research I thought that these stories would be the best source of material to construct a more comprehensive view of the afterlife as we can ascertain it from near death experiences. After reading through a few hundred stories I realized this may not be the case.

The reason for this has to do with the barrier. Kevin Williams has done an incredible amount of research into NDEs and has found that 46% of those having the experience will be come to a barrier. I came across this same phenomenon in my own research. Some describe an actual barrier and some are just told that they aren't ready. Some also come to the barrier and are told that they can cross it, but cannot come back to their lives on earth.

But the critical piece of information is that the barrier would of course lead us to believe that these people are not really in Heaven. They are in some kind of processing area. Within this area people have experiences that often align with their cultural or religious beliefs. I wanted to truly analyze the data in the same way I would sales data for a large retailer or manufacturing data. So I have to remove these outliers.

But then the children's stories kept popping up. They also have a barrier they cannot cross. Children as young as six years old aren't going to have a lot of cultural or religious influences. They also aren't going to be as creative as a thirty year old person who has spent years studying the bible or listening to a preacher in a church.

And yet these children have very vivid accounts and quite a lot of detail. To further complicate things, some adults, who aren't religious at all, and some who are even atheists have very detailed experiences that show the presence of angels or other divine beings.

All data is important so I used all of it for statistical purposes. But I also omitted some very detailed descriptions that may have better fleshed out Bob's experience. Instead I relied on stories that were duplicated often and had as little influence as possible from cultural or religious teachings. Was this the right approach? I can't say. Thankfully there is enough consistency between all of the stories that I don't think it greatly impacts my analysis on the nature of the experience.

Can you use the scientific method to prove the afterlife?

The study of near death experiences is often criticized because it doesn't follow the scientific method. This is interesting to me because it is largely untrue. The first step in just about any definition of the scientific method is that we should make observations. Then we begin to ask questions related to our observation and form hypothesis as to why this is happening.

This is precisely what I am doing and what many others are doing. It's just that we aren't through the process and we cannot separate the subjective. The key to the scientific method is in developing testable predictions that are objective and remove the subjective.

And this is where we are stuck. All of the observable information about the experience itself is subjective. This criticism has no integrity because that is the exact nature of the data as it presents. Subjective means personal perspectives or feelings. When subjective data is analyzed these personal opinions or perspectives are impossible to remove. There is no way to take a personal experience like an NDE and make it objective.

The most profound aspect of the NDE is the feeling of love. There is no way to make a feeling objective. But it's not just the feeling of love. When someone listens to a piece of music or looks at a beautiful work of art the experience is also subjective.

We can objectively identify every note and instrument in a work of classical music. But we cannot objectively describe the experience. The best that we can do is what I have done with Bob Fisher. Study thousands of people who like Beethoven's Fifth Symphony and catalogue their reasons. Then build a case that for most of the people who like a particular piece of music, this is the reason why. But we cannot get a complete understanding of the experience. It is subjective.

The further problem is we are trying to use a method of testing that may not be possible. All scientific testing revolves around variables and controls that are within our known physical universe. But the very nature of these near death experiences tells us that they happen outside the known three physical dimensions (and time), so the testing cannot work the same way.

So from a scientific standpoint, to create an objective theory about why these things happens may be possible.

To get to an objective answer of why and who also turns out to be nearly impossible.

We must find people who have had a life threatening event that caused the NDE to happen in the first place. And to be purely objective everyone should have had the same thing happen to them. This is why most of the studies revolve around heart attack patients. Everyone who has a heart attack and NDE now creates an objective base line. The problem here is that we eliminate most NDEs because they aren't caused by heart attacks, and yet the experiences are the same.

Even better (okay, actually worse) we need to find people at a high risk of dying, get them to join our research effort, hope they die but are then resuscitated. This is a fairly grim undertaking and not something that will incline people to volunteer.

The good news is that there doesn't seem to be a specific type of person who has an NDE. So at least we don't have to just find Christians who are going to have a heart attack. Everyone is a potential candidate. It's just that the people you select must be sick enough that they'll probably die and we can revive them long enough to talk to them about what they saw.

Given these limitations of any structured method the best that we can do is to make the observations, catalogue the data and then begin the process of analysis and development of a hypotheses to answer the question. And the question has been stuck on: "What is going on here?"

Why are we observing so many people who have a very similar experience that manifests itself on death or at least the very real fear of death?"

What I wanted to do that is a bit different is not worry so much about why this happened but instead focus on what happens.

These are two different things. For those who believe in God many already understand why it happens. We are near death and God or the angels, or some other spiritual being is preparing us for Heaven and our life after Earth.

So for those of us who believe in God we already know why it is happening, we just want to know what happens and if there is anything

that we can learn from the experience. For those who don't believe in God there is another theory that is emerging that says consciousness is caused by quantum mechanics. So even the atheist or agnostic will have some interest in the process of death and what happens to our consciousness.

If these questions are difficult to study that doesn't mean we stop. But I do think we need to look a bit beyond just figuring out the "why" of the question. With this book I spent much of my effort trying to figure out if the people who have an NDE have anything to tell us. Is God in some way using these people to send us a message? And how do we analyze that data to figure out what the message is?

The process I used to do this is similar to what the FBI or CIA might do to find terrorists. They gather hundreds of thousands or even millions of phone calls, texts and emails and try to find patterns that match a specific behavior.

The underlying problem with this approach is that you don't know what to look for until you see it and again the data is subjective.

When I first started building the database I scoured the internet, books and other forums and would download the data, put it in to a full text table with very little meta data and start looking for the things I already knew about, or that were already discussed somewhere else. But then I would read through five or six stories and by luck happen upon two of them that mention the tree. But when I tried to do the same thing with people who had seen pets it became much more difficult. Do I search on the word "pets" or "cats" or "dogs"? I did those three, and then came upon a horse. So now I had to add another search term about horses.

In the database I created I realized that I kept having to break down the data in to smaller and smaller experiences. To construct the narrative of Bob Fisher and Jim Stahlhaber I put each section into a chapter or paragraph of the book. By treating the different parts of the experience as their own dataset I was able to build a much clearer picture of what happens and what people see when they have an NDE.

To use a comprehensive and structured method, a scientific method, this creates other problems.

The biggest hurdle I had in analyzing the data and creating a structured process was without a doubt the out of body experience or OBE. The reason this is so challenging is that the out of body experience doesn't have a

religious or spiritual aspect to it in almost every single case I studied. It is completely separate from the spiritual or Heaven experience.

I even considered eliminating it from the book. There doesn't seem to be anything to learn about life from the out of body experience. But as I continued to read I found more and more people who said that their OBE was verified by a third party. And often verified by a disinterested party.

As you read through the first part of this book you may have noticed that this section seems somehow detached from the rest of the story. That is by design and it is because this is what the data suggested.

To further this research I decided to undertake a separate study of the OBE detached from the NDE. So I looked at the data of people who had an OBE but were not in a life threatening or near death situation. What I quickly found there was much less corroboration form third parties. So I didn't use any of that data in the book. It didn't fit with the process and it didn't offer enough consistency with those who had an OBE with a corresponding NDE.

Other parts that were broken down were the experience of seeing a city or a landscape. Some people describe a city, but don't have much to say about any forest, green grass or the big tree. Others see the forest, ponds, rolling green hills and the big tree but don't see a city.

By separating these experiences and analyzing them on their own I of course lose a little bit of integrity in the analysis. But that loss of integrity in the analysis actually builds a better description.

I thus am forced to start with a premise that the experience is real. I also start with the premise that not only is it real (meaning it actually happened to these people) but that it is what happens when we die.

By analyzing and constructing the data in this way I believe I've been able to create a much more descriptive and comprehensive picture of what we experience when we die.

To maintain as much integrity as possible I also had to remove those things that were statistically insignificant. Some of these statistically insignificant experiences are incredible. And they will also cause any researcher to let bias creep in.

In one particular story the person related seeing the gold lights before he had actually died. There are very few of these experiences where the spiritual and the initial Out of Body come together.

This is compelling. If this is true, it means that angels, or spirits, or whatever we want to call them, know before we do that we may not survive the ordeal. It suggests that before you suffer some horrible death an angel can jerk you out of your body and "save" you from the experience and just shuffle you straight in to Heaven.

That's a comforting thought. But there just aren't enough of those stories out there to make it statistically important or relevant. So Bob doesn't have that experience.

Does that mean it doesn't happen? No it doesn't. But if I'm going to try to keep the experience Bob has as honest as possible, I had to remove it.

This kind of thing happened quite a bit. And this demonstrates I think quite well the problem with using completely objective information to analyze what happens when we die. It cannot be done. People not only perceive identical events differently, they remember different aspects of the event. Why it happens may be able to be analyzed using the scientific method and there are as mentioned several working theories and ideas that are being tested. But I firmly believe they will all fall apart at the point where we are in a different dimension.

But there is even a bigger problem here that we must acknowledge. The atheist will always investigate the why of this in terms of the known universe without any regard for the supernatural. This is probably the best way to approach it, but it doesn't guarantee an answer. But those who are agnostic, or believe in God must face a different issue that is hard on our ego.

If the near death experience is a quick visit into the afterlife and heaven, and it is with or through God that this happens, we are never going to figure it out. If I believe in God, and that God created this entire universe then I must also admit that I am not going to outsmart God. The study of the Universe before the big bang is nearly impossible.

God could easily make the study of the afterlife impossible. We just can't get there from here. And God isn't going to let us. The data will only ever show us a glimpse and it will stop. If God created us, and we are to have free will it must always be this way.

Other theories about why NDE's happen

There are several theories floating around about why people have these profound experiences when they are close to death. Some of these theories are widely believed but have very big problems with them. One of the most recent revolves around the drug DMT. As part of my research I gathered some of the stories told by people who have taken this drug. There isn't nearly the breadth of information from those who take this drug, but it is a starting point and clearly shows some problems with this theory. The other two widely held theories revolve around an evolutionary trait or simply dreams or hallucinations caused by medications taking during the near death experience. And a more recent theory has been developed by physicist Roger Penrose and Stuart Hameroff an anesthesiologist. This theory revolves around consciousness and quantum mechanics.

Is the NDE an evolutionary trait?

The easiest of these theories to debunk, or at least offer a healthy dose of skepticism to is that the Near Death Experience is simply an evolutionary trait. So let us address this one first. I'll first acknowledge that I am a firm believer in evolution. I believe that as a species develops new traits some of these traits will lead to the expansion and survival of the species while others will be detrimental to the species.

If the NDE is a beneficial trait of the human species we can surmise of a logic behind this. If it is easier for the elderly of the species to die, then it

follows that there would be less competition for resources among those who remain. Thus the trait furthers the survival of the species.

There are few fundamental problems with this logic. Why would children have the experience? Wouldn't a trait that makes death not only easier, but by most accounts of those who have had an NDE wonderful, make it harder for the species to survive?

The other problem with this line of thinking is that every single one of the people who has experienced this wonderful bliss of death has decided to come back. Of course those who don't come back can't report the experience so that's more than a little tongue and cheek. But the reality is many are told they must go back, while others are allowed to decide from themselves.

If both of these can be explained away the third problem cannot. And it's one no one wants to address. According to a Gallup poll about 3% of Americans report having a near death experience. But many of these experiences are not of people going to a wonderful Heaven like afterlife, but instead going to Hell.

It is currently impossible to guess how many of these experiences end up with a vision of Hell or an experience of visiting Hell. But there are many.

The reason for this is probably pretty obvious. People are not inclined to tell you that they died and went to Hell. But suffice to say the Hell experience completely destroys the idea that the NDE is a beneficial evolutionary trait.

Does DMT, Ketamine or some other hallucinogenic drugs cause the NDE?

We can eliminate some drugs for two obvious reasons. The first is that these stories go back hundreds of years before these drugs had even been invented. The second is that of the thousands of documented stories about NDEs a large portion of them weren't in a hospital or under the influence voluntarily of a hallucinogenic drug.

That quickly leaves us with some kind of chemical that is already in the body and released at the time of the experience. Dimethyltryptamine or DMT is the chemical most widely credited with causing the NDE. It has been suggested by some that DMT is released by the pineal gland when one is close to death. I have not been able to find a single scientific study that

proves, or even suggests that this is true. It appears to be entirely speculative.

I still decided to investigate the phenomenon. As I mentioned earlier there aren't nearly as many people who have tried DMT as who have had a near death experience. So there just isn't much data to analyze.

The first thing I noticed was that many of the recorded experiences appear derivative of the writer Terrance McKenna.

The feeling of doing DMT is as though one had been struck by noetic lightning. The ordinary world is almost instantaneously replaced, not only with a hallucination, but a hallucination whose alien character is its utter alienness. Nothing in this world can prepare one for the impressions that fill your mind when you enter the DMT sensorium.

-Terence McKenna.

Heady stuff to be sure. But as you read through McKenna's experience and others who have taken the drug they don't seem to be anything at all like the near death experience. Although there are some consistencies between DMT experiences they don't mirror those NDE experiences in any meaningful way. As you read through the experiences you find that there are wild differences. Some people see aliens, others animals like crocodiles or lizards. Some people feel like they are in a dome and some feel like they are in outer space. The variances of experience make it nearly impossible to identify any internal data consistency that could be analyzed. While we may find at some point in the future that a chemical is causing the NDE it is hard for me to see any way that that it will be DMT.

Do dreams or comas account for NDEs?

This is an explanation that doesn't have a very wide following, but that I did run in to from time to time in my research. Let's dispel with comas first. We must separate comas with dreams because brain scans show that people who are in a coma do not have the same brain waves and patterns as someone who is sleeping. Thus they are not likely to be dreaming. There are however some people who have been in comas who report nightmares or other experiences similar to dreams.

Normal sleep/wake cycle dreams do have some consistency to them. But people don't report having the same dreams after a similar experience in the way that NDEs manifest themselves.

As you dive deeper in to the near death experience there is something else that is quite extraordinary. During the "Life Review" people relate that they can feel what

the other person was feeling at the time of the incident being reviewed. If you treated someone badly you can feel what they feel. Now I of course cannot analyze or study every dream anyone has ever had, I have never heard of this before about a dream.

Penrose and Hameroff. Orchestrated objective reduction Orch-OR theory

This theory is certainly very interesting. Roger Penrose is a brilliant physicist and an atheist. Hameroff is a medical doctor, an anesthesiologist and believes in God and the spiritual nature of consciousness.

In Hameroff's own words;

"My research involves a theory of consciousness which can bridge these two approaches, a theory developed over the past 20 years with eminent British physicist Sir Roger Penrose. Called 'orchestrated objective reduction' ('Orch OR'), it suggests consciousness arises from quantum vibrations in protein polymers called microtubules inside the brain's neurons, vibrations which interfere, 'collapse' and resonate across scale, control neuronal firings, generate consciousness, and connect ultimately to 'deeper order' ripples in space-time geometry. Consciousness is more like music than computation"

When we look at this theory from the perspective of both Penrose and Hameroff (again one an atheist and another who believes in God) it raises a question that is actually kind of funny. If our consciousness continues after we die due to quantum mechanics, what is happening when we die?

If the theory is true, the atheist would say, we don't really die, we are just in another state of consciousness and in another dimension that we don't yet understand. While the more spiritual would say that we are in Heaven. And the Orch-OR theory is just what God uses to get us there, or how it works when we are in Heaven.

The religious today are branded as Luddites who don't value or understand science. To suggest that Hameroff is a Luddite is patently ridiculous. But the truth is, he isn't an outlier. Most Christians that I know believe in evolution, and believe that the universe is billions of years old. They just happen to believe that evolution is the way God works.

This theory has not, and with current science cannot be completely tested and verified. It is perhaps more interesting to me as a computer

programmer because it certainly breaks any correlation between how the brain works and how computers work.

What happens when we die?

If the Gallup poll from 1982 is correct and 3% of United States citizens have said they have had a Near Death Experience we can probably assume that the percentage is the same across all seven billion people on Earth. That's 210 million people who have had a Near Death Experience. With all of those people having the experience, and thousands of them being documented at some level, what can we learn about dying?

Before going into this I also need to clarify that there are quite a bit of subtle differences between them. But there is a fairly consistent process.

You will float above your body.
The experience often starts with an out of body experience. You will float above your body and feel detached. You will be able to see yourself and others around you. You may see your family and friends standing over you. Slowly you will be pulled away and go through a tunnel or feel like you are traveling through the universe. You will see little stars or points of light zipping past you.

Then you will find yourself in a bright light. This light will be brighter than the sun but it will not hurt your eyes. The light may feel very warm to you. A comforting warmth to be sure. You will feel very calm and peaceful. You will not be afraid of dying and may welcome it at this point.

What I found most interesting in my research surrounding the out of body experience is that it is not spiritual. There seems to be a line between

the out of body experience right after death, and the experience of either Heaven or Hell. There were a few cases I came across where people were revived right after the out of body, floating experience. It is only when this experience is ending that people have a religious or spiritual near death experience.

The spirits and loved ones.

You will see spirits or angels. They are usually just gold forms with undistinguishable faces. They may just be glowing orbs but some may be wearing brilliant white gowns. You will also see people you know who have already died. You will see friends, parents, grandparents and other relatives. Some of them may tell you that you have to go back. That it isn't your time. Even though they are very happy to see you, if it is not your time they will tell you to go back. You will communicate with these people and spirits instantly. You won't have to speak and you won't necessarily hear them talking with your ears. But the communication will be clear and instant.

You may understand everything.

You may not have any questions. You may understand everything. It will be so clear to you that you won't even think of the word "logic". It will just be, and you will understand it. This was difficult to put into words in the book because so many who have the experience say they cannot put it into words. It's just natural and normal for them to understand everything. I think this is why so few people come back having ask questions. They already know all of the answers. There are others who do have questions and have ask God, "What is the meaning of life?" Some say, "Love is the meaning of life." Others say they cannot remember, but knew at the time. But quite a few say they understood everything.

You will see a landscape.

The landscape will be filled with trees, brilliant green grass and flowers like you have never seen before. You will be able to rapidly move from place to place by just looking at the area or the thing you want to see. The landscape is similar to earth but will be much brighter and more colorful.

You now come to the city.

The city will be made of gold and other precious gems and it will be perfect. There will be plants and flowers and streams in the city. But nature and the buildings will fit together perfectly. You will see people and spirits inside the city. The city will appear to be alive and light will come from everything.

Then you have your life review.

You will have a review of your entire life. It will be shown either on one big screen or a bunch of smaller televisions. You will experience what other people felt when you interacted with them. There may be others with you watching your life review. You will not be judged and you will not judge yourself.

You will see or feel a barrier.

Then you will either cross that barrier or return to Earth.

If you cross the barrier, no one has any idea what it will be like. We just know for sure that no one has ever been to the barrier, crossed over and come back.

ABOUT THE AUTHOR

Eric Gurr is a data analyst and computer programmer from Hamilton, Ohio. He has been married for 31 years and has three children and 3 grandchildren. He lives with his wife on a small lavender farm in Madison Township Ohio.

Eric can be reached for comments or questions and for speaking engagements at

gurreric@gmail.com